'This is Afric⋯ ⋯ ⋯are seldom seen alone, ei⋯ ⋯g or in hotels.'

'How old-fashioned!' said Angela with a hint of irritation.

'We care for our women here,' he replied.

'But you are French, and surely the French are one of the most liberated countries in the world. You can't have that archaic opinion!'

'It depends on the woman,' Jean-Louis said calmly. 'And I consider myself to be Tunisian. But I have a better and more practical idea,' he continued in a voice that showed he had made up his mind that she would agree. 'I will fly you to Bizerta and show you a typical Tunisian village.'

'I couldn't possibly ask you to waste your time on . . .a complete stranger,' she said, and had the satisfaction of seeing him incline his head and give an ironic smile.

'But I feel that we do know each other, Sister,' he said smoothly. 'I am not being generous. I shall expect something in return.'

Lisa Cooper was brought up on the Isle of Wight and went to a well-known London teaching hospital to train as a nurse. After a short spell as a theatre sister, she married an accountant, and their two children also have medical connections, her son being a biologist with a pharmaceutical firm and her daughter a medical scientist in a famous hospital for sick children.

Lisa Cooper feels it is important to show the complete professional integrity of the hero and heroine as well as their deep-felt emotions, and she makes a point of carefully researching latest developments in surgery and medical science. Writing as a second career began at home when she was unable to go back to nursing in hospital, and she has now written over thirty books.

Previous Titles

FLOWERS FOR WARD SIX
AMSTERDAM ENCOUNTER
THE RIGHT TO LIFE

EASTERN ADVENTURE

BY

LISA COOPER

MILLS & BOON LIMITED
ETON HOUSE   18–24 PARADISE ROAD
RICHMOND   SURREY   TW9 1SR

First published in Great Britain 1990 by Mills & Boon Limited

© Lisa Cooper 1990

Australian copyright 1990
Philippine copyright 1991
This edition 1991

ISBN 0 263 77109 1

Set in 10½ on 12 pt Linotron Times
03-9101-50227
Typeset in Great Britain by Centracet, Cambridge
Made and printed in Great Britain

CHAPTER ONE

'THAT'S wonderful!' said Sister Angela Menzies. 'He'll be over the moon with relief.'

She put the folder down on the desk and looked up, slightly puzzled. 'Are you sure I have the right patient?' she asked, with a slight smile. 'I was booked for six weeks to look after a serious case, and now he'll be able to go out in four or five days.'

'We have to make sure a case is covered,' said Wendy, the hospital secretary. 'And Miss Pritchard who does all the admissions told us to expect a man to come in for exploration—probably laparotomy and a major operation on the gut,' she added, consulting the notes again.

'So here I am with a patient I've met once to get him ready for X-ray and who now needs me like he needs a sore thumb after hearing that his barium meal and follow-through are negative! He has a slight diverticulitis that can be controlled and maybe even cured by diet and light medication.'

'You'll have to make sure that he understands his diet and treatment,' suggested Wendy.

'That will take about half a day,' said Angela. 'So I suppose Miss Pritchard will tactfully tell me I'm no longer required, and I'll have to ring the agency to see if there's any other work for me.' She wrinkled her nose, then laughed. 'Maybe not. She has a reputation for clinging on to agency nurses once she has them here, and Sister Crane says she gives out case histories like library books, without bothering to ask if a nurse has any experience of the work required. I doubt if she knows anything much about surgery or medicine and cares even less. She never visits the patients unless they complain about the food or noise from the building works up the road, but rumour has it that she *does* play bridge with the VIPs.'

'It's her job to look impressive and to give the hospital a bit of style. After all, we have some of the most important people here—pop stars, famous athletes and even Members of Parliament,' said Wendy. 'She doesn't have to know about disease, but makes sure they're comfortable and shunts them out with a smile and the hefty bill that this private hospital charges.'

'Well, I hope she hands me an interesting library book,' said Angela. 'To be honest, I thought I'd earn more money by working privately, and I'm saving up for something special, but if I don't work, I don't get paid.'

Wendy regarded her with a mixture of admiration and curiosity. 'Money is important,' she agreed.

'That's one aspect of going private that I hate. In my old training hospital up north, I just got on with my work and did my best for everyone, and we all worked together and had loads of laughs.' Angela's voice tailed away and a wave of homesickness made her feel suddenly miserable. She smoothed down the well-fitting uniform dress over her slim hips and straightened the dark blue belt at her tiny waist.

She frowned. 'Working for the agency is interesting and I admit I enjoy the extras it brings and the good conditions here, but I have the feeling that patients are rushed in and out and have to go home before they can really cope with everyday living. It doesn't matter who they are, they all suffer from post-operative weakness, and yet some are sent home before their stitches are out. I suppose they have the GP's surgery nurse to remove them.'

Wendy laughed. 'I can see you're new here! You have to be joking! Anyone who can afford the fees here has staff at home to pander to their every whim. This is another world, Sister. It has no comparison with the home conditions of patients you met in your training school in a depressed area.'

'They have something in common,' said Angela softly. 'They've all suffered, physically and mentally. Pain brings everyone down to the same level, and emotional crises have no barriers.'

Wendy picked up the folder and paused when she reached the door of the office. 'Nice to know someone with a few illusions,' she said, but she wondered how long it would be before the efficient and attractive new sister would be influenced by the wealth and force of the men, women and children who passed beyond the ornate doors of reception.

'I'm having coffee now, and you might as well have yours here too,' Angela offered. 'I expect some of the others will come in later, but they're all busy with their patients just now.'

Wendy eyed her as she poured coffee from the fine porcelain pot and wondered if the move from a downbeat area in the north had had a traumatic affect on this girl with such sleek thick blonde hair and wide green eyes. The delicate features showed sensitivity and the slightly wide mouth was generous and soft. 'Why did you come here, really?' she asked.

'I finished my midwifery and suddenly had no plans.' Angela gave a bright smile that almost reached her eyes but not quite. 'I thought I'd save up and go travelling, being footloose and fancy-free, as they say.'

'Anywhere in particular?'

Angela hesitated. From experience, she had learned that secretaries often gossiped as much as nurses did, and it was unwise to say anything that might be spread about the place if it was something she wanted to keep to herself.

She smiled. As she had no lurid skeletons locked away in her past there was no harm in giving a little, but to the girl listening, her secret smile seemed to hide the real reason for her desire to travel. 'I have to get to Tunisia,' Angela admitted. 'I want to see someone there.'

'Tunisia? Just wait around here for a while. The clinic is full of rich Arabs and other Middle Eastern people.'

'I don't want to work there. I want to save enough to go there on holiday,' Angela said.

'You'll come back?' The sidelong glance was sharp and knowing, and Angela bubbled with inner laughter.

'Who knows?' she said slowly. The girl was obviously putting all the wrong ideas together, and by suppertime she would be convinced that the new sister had a mysterious lover in North Africa. What did it matter? Angela wondered. Every hospital had its own grapevine of gossip that was the lifeblood of the social community, and everyone shared the news and scandal and romance that came to a large establishment staffed by mainly attractive people.

'Boyfriend?' ventured Wendy.

'Shall we say that I'm hoping to see someone very dear to me? But to get back to business, what do I do now? Has dear Gwladys Pritchard, our manager, anything lined up for me after I've waved goodbye to my patient and had my day off, the day after tomorrow?'

Wendy consulted a sheet of paper from her print-out. 'There are three patients coming in today, but you can't take any of them as they need immediate nursing. Tomorrow we have two more, one bringing his own nursing sister, who'll have the room next to his while he undergoes tests. Money no object!' She shrugged. 'Three for X-ray in Outpatients, and the place will be full except for the three emergency beds which are empty, so you may have to pack your bags!'

Angela groaned. 'That's the disadvantage of this job. I hate the idea of being shunted out to a private chronic case in darkest Bucks or Surrey to relieve a nurse on leave. I think I shall go off the whole idea if that's all I'm offered, and meekly return to a badly paid job with lots of interest, in the NHS.'

She glanced at the shining digital clock that relentlessly ticked away the life of the hospital and felt a pang of regret for her old training school. It might have lacked décor and had a very draughty out-patients' department, but the shabby corridors exuded warmth, comfort and friendliness. This place was bright and comfortable, gleaming clean, and gave a very efficient service, as she knew from the glowing reports from doctors who she knew had used the hospital for their private cases, but she now sensed why most nurses went to other jobs once they had worked in the busy smart place for a while.

'Thanks for coffee. If you're going to see your patient, would you take these papers up to Sister Simmons on the way?' asked Wendy.

Angela walked along the pale green corridor, her slim white leather pumps sinking into the deep carpet. Windowsills held beautiful floral arrangements, and she bent to catch the scent from some magnificent carnations that couldn't possibly have been grown in England during the bleak March weather. The feathery ferns moved on her breath and she sighed. This kind of luxury must give a lot of pleasure to all who walked along the corridors.

'Damn things!' said a male voice. 'Give me hay fever.' The doctor grinned and passed by quickly. His bulky figure and badly fitting suit made him an incongruous figure in the smart clinic, but Angela knew that he was perhaps the leading authority on allergic diseases, and being a genius he could afford to look like a tramp!

As she walked to the lift, she wondered if men who took just a little too much care of their appearance might be lacking in some way, and a sudden vision of Patrick flashed before her mind. She bit her lip. I'm just a coward, she decided. He was a safe distance away now and she could ignore the many telephone calls and letters that he now sent, begging her to marry him and to forgive and forget that he had ever tried to force her to have sex with him.

Patrick. . .with that fatal charm and that soft Irish accent and the smooth persuasion that had almost convinced her that it would be wonderful to move in with him to the small service flat behind the old hospital.

Her chin jutted defiantly, as far as a small chin with a dimple in the middle could jut. He can have his adoring harem! she thought. He can notch up his conquests, but he'll never add me to his score. Away from his charm, she knew that the attraction she had felt so deeply was only physical and that his studied and immaculate appearance was a disguise for lack of moral strength and inner generosity of spirit. She gave a low laugh. At least she had damaged that image when he'd tried to rape her. She'd slapped him hard, kneed him where it hurt most and told him she never wanted to see him again.

The carpet on the second floor was pale pink,

echoing the pearly walls, and the scent of air freshener was subtle enough to blend with the fresh flowers. A door, a few yards from the lift, was open and she saw that the office was empty. She walked in slowly, putting the notes on the desk. If she took them along to the room where Mr Macintosh was resting, Sister Simmons would not see the notes when she returned to the office, so they were better left where she couldn't miss them as she needed the report.

The whole department was quiet, even where the carpet gave way discreetly to tiles of the same colour and bare walls with no flowers on the sills, at the point where the surgical department began and the way to the superbly equipped operating theatre needed easy cleanliness and stark efficiency.

Sister Simmons emerged from the double doors of the theatre. She was smiling and adjusting her cap. 'Sister Menzies? Just the person I wanted to see.' She led the way to the office. 'I heard about your patient, so we needn't go into that now.' She dismissed Mr Macintosh as if he were a pound of sugar she was returning to the store. 'We have trouble,' she stated with great satisfaction. 'I was so bored with varicose veins and hernias, but now something really interesting has cropped up.'

'Something for me?' asked Angela.

Sister Simmons eyed the eager expression and the sparkling green eyes and laughed. 'Could well be,' she said as if she had a private joke. 'Have you ever heard of Shane Winsconsin?'

'The racing driver?'

'The same! He came off the track during a practice run. He says the track was greasy after rain and he blames himself for thinking he could get away with the wrong tyres. The car was scheduled for a race later this month and he was testing something.'

'Is he badly hurt?' Angela recalled the TV pictures of a compactly built man with wild hair, wasting perfectly good champagne in a shaken froth as he sat on the back of a car, wearing a wreath of flowers round his neck.

'One fractured leg and some abrasions: not enough to worry anyone but enough to keep him away in here safe from the Press for a week or so.'

Angela raised her eyebrows. 'So, in here, no Press are allowed to interview him?'

'You get the picture. That's one of the reasons why it's so popular. We've kept cabinet ministers and film stars safe from harassment here, and it pays. Sometimes, famous people aren't really ill but come here for a rest and peace, if they can afford the time and money.'

'You said we have trouble? That doesn't sound like trouble to me. Rather fun, in fact,' said Angela.

'Fun he may be, but trouble is what I meant. He's not only got a death wish on the track, but he's a womaniser. I'm just warning you that he'll make a pass at you and probably grope you when you make his bed.'

'Thanks very much,' said Angela drily. 'Do I get danger money? Do I abandon Mr Macintosh entirely and nurse your pet celebrity?'

'Not altogether. You can help out with both of them, as they only need the odd bell answered and a bit of chat to keep them from dying of boredom.'

'Just feed them coffee and comforting words and tuck them in at night? Sounds a doddle, except for when I have to do a bed bath and rub Shane Winsconsin's pressure points! Does this mean I stay here for a while? Does Miss Pritchard know and approve?' The horrors of nursing one patient out in the backwoods receded.

'Yes to all that. Shane will be under traction for the leg, so he can't chase you round the room at present.'

'He sounds manic! How do you know so much about him?' Angela asked.

Sister Simmons laughed. 'He was in here for plastic surgery about a year ago after burns and he wasn't confined to bed all the time, so we know his little ways. He's great fun if you can handle him, and I think you can.' She noted the calm unhurried grace and hoped that the cool blonde could freeze the ebullient racing driver.

'Thanks for warning me,' laughed Angela. 'I shall escape to Mr Macintosh when I need to if the atmosphere gets fraught.'

'I think you can say we need you for a while,' said Sister. 'There's another case coming in soon. I've alerted theatre as it's an emergency, so all our spare beds will be full. This is a child for eye surgery, and her mother will stay with her in the last room we have vacant.' She glanced at some notes. 'A child of ten with a piece of metal in one eye. Her own surgeon will be doing it and using our electro-magnetic extractor. They're Middle-Eastern, and even with her mother hovering over her you'll be needed for any aftercare that's required.'

'It's just as well I have eye ward experience,' Angela said. 'But I suppose every trained nurse has a fairly comprehensive knowledge of all branches of care.'

'You'd be surprised,' Sister Simmons stated shortly. 'That's why the agency is fussy who they have on their books. Some hospitals just transfer their specialist cases to bigger centres, and the poor nurses never get a glimpse of them if there's no unit, for example, for eyes or allergies, and some of the newer transplant surgery.'

'We had a good eye unit where I trained and I enjoyed working there. Is the injury serious?' It was better to concentrate on the unknown child than to look back with longing to her old life.

'We don't yet know. The theatre is laid up for everything from the magnet to complete enuclea-tion.' Sister Simmons shuddered. 'I hate eye sur-gery, and it would be tragic if a young girl had to lose an eye at such an early age.' She glanced along the empty corridor. 'When you go down for meals, please make no reference to this case. In fact, it's as well not to talk about any of the people here.'

Angela nodded, but was surprised. It had been stressed quite forcefully when she first came to the hospital that privacy and secrecy were as important as treatment, and yet Sister Simmons seemed to think that this case was even more secret. Everyone knew that a leak to the Press about any patient would lead to instant dismissal.

'I'm not being extra fussy,' Sister explained. 'There may be newspaper reporters and cameramen hanging about trying to get an interview with the child's mother and father. They're members of a foreign diplomatic circle, and the splinter of metal was a direct result of an attempt on the life of the father.'

Angela gasped. 'Do you think they're safe here?'

'The father has returned to his own country, and that fact is known to the Press. The attack was made yesterday, but it was thought it wasn't safe to take the child home for surgery as there were places here that could do everything necessary, and their own man is available here. Even by private jet it would have taken hours and been very tiring for the poor little mite. I believe they would also have a long car drive at the other end, and of course, London is a famous centre for eye surgery. They kept her quietly in a private house last night, and today she'll be brought here, incognito.'

'Have we a guard on the door? Surely there may still be danger for the family, even if the father has left the UK.' Angela thought the corridor was far too empty and vulnerable. What if a kidnap attempt was made?

Sister Simmons seemed to share her unease. 'The porters downstairs know most of the reporters who lurk about the hospital, and Wendy at her desk can smell them a mile away. The button in my office calls security and we have a very good retired police

officer on call, but Wendy is off duty this evening
and so am I, so be very careful who comes and goes
in case anyone slips past the relief girl in reception.'

'I shall have to answer bells in my other two
rooms, Sister,' Angela reminded her.

'There will be a reliable ward maid on duty who
does drinks and light snacks for visitors. She can
watch from the kitchen and will look out if she hears
a bell, to cover the corridor and the lift. The other
sisters will be around, but it's your job to see that
nobody goes into the rooms used by the ben Ksar
family or into Shane's room. The papers are dying
to get to him.'

'Could I have a list of people allowed access? If I
know names, I can more easily refuse admission to
anyone not on the list,' suggested Angela.

'I'd almost forgotten—I do have a list ready.
Quite easy today, as Shane isn't allowed any visitors
at all as we suspect he might suffer some delayed
surgical shock. He was pretty shaken, and having to
have emergency surgery is a strain for even a man
of his physique. The office will vet all phone calls,
so that leaves him isolated for a while.'

'And the child?'

'Aysha will have her mother with her, and she'll
tell you who's allowed to visit them later, but just
now they'll have only the surgeon and other medical
staff in that room.' Sister's face was serious, and her
concern was infectious.

'I didn't know I'd be made head of security,'
Angela ventured with a tight smile. 'If this care is
needed, then thank heavens I'm not rich or famous!

Do I know all the doctors? Anyone can wear a white coat!'

'You know them all except for the surgeon who will operate on Aysha. It's probably the man from Guy's, who's short and stocky and going bald at the back. Everyone here knows him.'

'And if I see any dark foreign-looking men looking for room seven?'

'You ring security on the panic button and try to bleep the common-room to alert the staff. Stall all questions if someone gets through on the internal phone, and the theatre will let you know when Aysha is due back from her op. I'm putting her in room seven, next to Shane in room eight, to make it simpler for you. The walking case didn't mind moving as his new room has a better view of the park.'

'Would that be Aysha now, being admitted?' Angela listened intently. The soft whine of the lift was barely discernible and the gentle clop of the doors was as discreet as a breeze. A stretcher trolley was pushed rapidly past the two nursing sisters, the face of the patient hidden under a cloche of metal and plastic, designed to shield against the weather when the patient was transferred from ambulance to hospital. Angela glanced out of the window. The weather was clear and cool but dry, and she realised that the cover was there to protect the girl from prying eyes and not against the weather. It must be serious, to keep her identity so secret.

A tall man with broad shoulders bent over the

trolley, steadying the child's head gently and murmuring to her. He wore a light overcoat of vicuña
and the back of his head was muffled under a pale
grey silk scarf. A woman held one of the small
hands of the child on the trolley. As Angela stepped
back to let the trolley pass, she wondered if the face
matched the strength and good lines of the man's
body, and she wanted to see that face. The loose
coat brushed her bare arm almost like a caress and
she was aware of the male force that now had gone
as the doors of the theatre annexe opened and
closed behind the small procession, hiding him from
view and further speculation.

'He's new,' said Sister Simmons. 'Probably a
relative or someone from the Embassy.'

The woman who had walked with the trolley now
came slowly towards them. Her long black hair was
skilfully coiffured, but the delicate beauty of the
dark eyes and darkly red lips was blurred by anxiety.
She raised an appealing glance to Sister Simmons
and tears formed in the lovely eyes. 'Who will help
me with my Aysha?' she asked.

'Sister Menzies will be here all the evening, and
you may ask her for anything you need, *madame*,'
said Sister Simmons. 'I haven't met your surgeon.
Do you know him well?'

She can't ask if he's competent, thought Angela,
but she knew that the thought was in Sister
Simmons' mind too.

'He is good, and he came to help us because he is
kind and knows us well. After, he must leave, and

then who will help me with my child? I have many servants but no skilled nurses,' said the woman.

'Your doctor will advise you,' suggested Angela. 'You may be able to leave here in a day or so, and he'll know what is best for Aysha.'

'I would like you,' said Madame ben Ksar. Her dark eyes were calculating. 'I need you to look after my child,' she added imperiously.

'I will do all I can while you're here, but I have other patients to attend to,' Angela pointed out gently. 'Come and sit down and I'll bring you some coffee. You must be exhausted,' she added kindly.

'You are good.' The slender brown hand fluttered over Angela's wrist. 'I know that you will be kind.'

When she came with the coffee, in a pretty pot on a tray with a tiny vase of flowers and a delicate assortment of small cakes, Angela saw that Madame ben Ksar was drained of all spirit. She persuaded her to eat and drink and to recline on the day-bed, and when the maid came to take the tray Angela was able to leave her half asleep while she went to check with her other patients.

Mr Macintosh was in a very good mood. 'I thought I was for the chop, Sister. They say I can go home tomorrow. If I have to eat brown bread for the rest of my life, so be it,' he added piously. 'I hate the stuff, but it'll be a small price to pay for good health.'

'There's more to the diet than brown bread, and you do have a lot of choice. Here's a diet sheet and suggestions for full meals. Very appetising, and *very* good for you,' Angela said with a smile.

'I'll study this now, Sister. I know how busy you are, and I don't think I'll want anything before my next meal.'

It was a relief to have a cheerful patient. It made life easy, she thought as she hesitated at the door of room eight where Shane Winsconsin was now in bed. Surely he couldn't be the menace that Sister Simmons thought him to be? She tapped on the door and opened it slowly, the light from the corridor making a halo of her fair hair in the dim light of the room.

Shane was dozing but lifted one eyelid as she came to the bedside. He moved and winced as she pulled at the leg under traction. 'Hell, I'm thirsty,' he said.

Angela glanced at his chart. She poured out a carefully measured amount of orange juice into a feeding cup.

'I don't mean that muck,' he grumbled. 'I want a proper drink. I want lashings of really cold beer or a pint of champagne.' His eyes challenged her.

'I go by your chart, Mr Winsconsin,' she replied crisply. 'So far you've been sick twice because you drank your juice too fast.'

'Are you surprised? That muck is guaranteed to make you throw up! Get me a pint of real ale and you won't see that again, Nursey dear,' he said with an insolent smile, noting her clear skin, the firm breasts and the long slim legs. She offered the cup again, as if he was a tiresome child requiring patience. He took the cup and tried to imprison her hand, but she slipped away. 'Know it all, huh?' he remarked. His eyes were bold. 'I might have guessed. With that chassis, you're bound to run into trouble in the pits.'

Angela looked amused but not annoyed. It was easy to see the effect he might have on teenage groupies, but her complete detachment made him sip the orange juice slowly and look vaguely embarrassed.

A bell purred and she adjusted his pillows, assured him that she would be back to wash him later and left the room. A flurry of activity by the lift told her that the trolley had gone down to collect dispensary and dressings for the theatre. That must mean that Aysha's operation was over. She hurried to room seven and saw a small form lying on the bed with both eyes bandaged. Madame ben Ksar sat by the bed, tears in her eyes, and Angela went to her and touched her shoulder in a gesture of comfort. She murmured words of reassurance, and sensed rather than saw the presence of a man at the door, but as she turned the shadow had gone, and she dismissed it as a trick of the light, but shivered, with a faintly sensual impression that eyes that held warmth had been regarding her. Her body responded to something intangible; less than a touch, more than a glance. I didn't even see him, she thought, but I know he has dark, dark eyes.

Sister Simmons came in briefly to look at the chart, and asked Angela to come to the office. 'Sister Menzies, I don't know what plans you've made, but as far as the agency is concerned there's been a change,' she said. 'I've had Miss Pritchard on the phone insisting that you be relieved of all duties other than looking after the eye case.'

'But Aysha has her mother there, and apart from dressings there'll be little to do for her,' objected Angela.

'Madame ben Ksar wants you exclusively, and who are we to argue with all that wealth and influence?'

'What did they find in theatre?' Angela asked.

'A nasty piece of metal which was removed by magnet, safely with no further injury. Theatre Sister was impressed by the surgeon and said he's quite as good as Russell from Guy's. He's also a friend of the family and says that Aysha will have the bandages off in two days' time, and your job will be four-hourly irrigations and eye-pads, until the dressings are abandoned for good.'

'So there will be some treatment to do,' said Angela with relief.

'After that you go with them when they leave here,' Sister added.

'To the Embassy?'

'I hope your passport is in order,' said Sister Simmons drily. She laughed. 'Don't look so alarmed! You'll need it if you go to Tunisia, and a little bird told me you wanted to go there. Now you go for free! Why not send him a cable? You'll travel with the family in a private jet and have your fees paid all the time you're with them. Some girls have all the luck! Any questions?'

'No.' Angela's head was in a whirl. A flood of excitement made her eyes tender. Dear Dermot! He was only a half-brother, but he was all she had and very precious. If only he wouldn't insist on burying himself in out-of-the-way places like phosphate mining camps in the Middle East!

'Do what shopping you need and pack to be ready in two days' time,' she heard Sister Simmons say.

A bell rang and she forced her attention to the present. A man was walking along the corridor away from the stairs by the lift as if he didn't want to be noticed. Sister Simmons had gone into one of the rooms and Angela was alone. The man hesitated outside the room where Aysha was sleeping, then went on to the door marked eight. Angela took a deep breath. A reporter! He was looking for Shane Winsconsin. What cunning! He was dressed in a white shirt and loose trousers as if he had every right to be there. By now, Wendy had left her desk, the porter might be bringing even more flowers to the upper floor and it was the one hour when security was at its weakest.

She ran along the corridor, making little sound, but the man turned just as his hand was raised to tap on the door. She saw his face for the first time and her breath caught on a rough barrier in her throat. Her heart made strange flutterings and she stopped running. A white smile in a sun-tanned face and the hooded eyes showed full approval. His voice was low and full and musical. 'Perhaps you could find out if he is awake?' he suggested.

'You can't go in there. I have orders to stop anyone from entering that room,' she insisted.

'I came to see Aysha, but she is asleep, so until

she has her evening treatment I'm going to visit a friend.' He laughed softly. 'Do you always defend your patients as fiercely, Sister?'

'How do I know you are his friend? You might be a reporter,' Angela said accusingly.

'I'm an old friend of Shane's and we've driven together, and I want to see him.' The voice took on a more steely edge, and Angela turned the door-handle, opened the door slightly and saw that Shane was asleep.

She closed the door quickly. 'He's asleep,' she said. 'There's no point in going in if you can't talk to him.'

'I want to see him,' he said mildly. Angela found herself lifted into the air and swung casually away from the door. The grip on her waist was firm yet gentle, as if she was part of a dance. She looked down into the dark eyes, conscious of the thin material of her uniform dress and the tight line of her bikini pants across her hips. His hands slid upwards as she came down to the floor and he held her lightly, close to his body. Her eyelids fluttered and hid her deep unease. The soft curve of her breast was warm against the silk shirt and the warmth flickered into flame. She pushed away and nearly fell, making him hold her more closely.

'Please let me go,' she pleaded. Who was this man who could reduce her to helplessness at their first meeting? But was it the first meeting? He went to the bedside and grinned.

'Poor old Shane! I'll come back later. I think I shall see you again too, Sister.'

'No!' She blushed. 'I mean, it's unlikely, as I'm going away with a patient. I don't know who you are, but please check with Sister Simmons before you try to visit again. I had no right to allow you into that room.'

'You didn't.' He took her hand and kissed the curling fingers. 'You tried most bravely to stop me, and I forced myself on you.' His voice was mocking. He drew her swiftly towards him and kissed her lips. 'There, now you can run to Sister Simmons, breathing fire and offended dignity.' He pushed her gently into the room and closed the door. Shaking, Angela opened the door again, but the corridor was empty.

CHAPTER TWO

'WE ARE nearly there!' Madame ben Ksar was excited. She smiled at the English nursing sister who sat beside her on the plane circling Tunis Airport and looked fondly at the child who snuggled up to her new friend and nurse, the small head resting on Angela's bosom and the exposed eye drooping with sleep.

The Tunisian woman now became the confident one, in charge of the situation. 'I am going home, but you are the stranger here and must feel at a loss.' She laughed softly. 'It will be Aysha leading you, and not you taking her hand to give her courage as you did in London.'

'It all happened so soon,' said Angela. 'I've hardly caught my breath.' Yesterday was a dream, the day before was an era gone in which a memory that disturbed her had gone as if it had never been, and she wanted to put a hand back to London to make sure she had packed everything she needed and had turned off the heater in her flat.

She stared out of the oval window and tried to forget the mocking smile, the touch of a man's mouth on hers and the guilty response that her body had made to his sexuality. It meant nothing, she told herself sternly, and a casual laughing kiss could happen to anyone and be something over which to smile later, but she was not smiling.

The plane dipped lower and the countryside unfolded like a relief map as Tunis town came into sight. The shadow of the wings swept over flat white-roofed houses, ignored by unconcerned people in *djellabas*; people who might never fly but who now accepted the constant flow of air traffic as unremarkable as the orange trees flourishing in every village and along the roads between towns. Glimpses of flooded fields and mud-spattered walls came with the outline of huge apartment blocks and the university buildings that Madame ben Ksar pointed out when Angela exclaimed at the modern appearance of the city.

'Forget everything you have heard about our country,' she said. 'If you try to analyse it you will go crazy. We live in the deep past and in the future, and we are surprisingly civilised!' she laughed, and the gentle teasing note was one that Angela had grown to love. Vassila ben Ksar took no offence at any condescending remarks about her country, but turned them aside with skill and humour and a certain pride. She still wore the smart clothes that fitted into the London scene, and Aysha looked like any schoolgirl from any country, a pretty child with dark hair and eyes and a clear skin the colour of warm coffee cream.

'*Nous sommes arrivés*,' said Vassila, lapsing into French, the second language of the family after Arabic. Angela blessed the fact that she had a working knowledge of French, but blenched at the thought of learning Arabic.

'With Angela I must speak English,' Aysha said slowly. She smiled and the protective eye-patch seemed unimportant. 'You will come riding with me, Angela?'

'No riding until Jean-Louis gives permission,' Vassila said.

Angela fumbled with the catch of her flight bag and her mouth was suddenly dry. Jean-Louis Joudet, the French doctor who had kissed her, was far away in London. 'Now you are home again, I suppose you must ask your own doctor,' she ventured.

'Jean-Louis is our doctor and a good friend. Perhaps not, as you say, a GP. Is that right? He is skilful and kind, and Aysha loves him as an uncle.' Madame shrugged as if that made it reasonable to expect the leading eye surgeon in Tunisia to come at her bidding if her daughter caught a cold, had a fever or sprained her ankle. She looked at Angela more closely. 'I forget. Did you meet him? I didn't see you in our room when he visited, and he did the first dressing himself when you were off duty and Sister Simmons was there.'

'I saw him briefly,' Angela said. She kept her voice level. 'I expect he's busy in London. Does he have a big clinic there?'

'He has cases there at times, but not now, I think. The Embassy called him to us and he came,' Madame said casually.

'His home is here?' The dread of meeting him

again made Angela feel cold. She licked her lips and was afraid her voice was husky. This is ridiculous, she thought. A man laughed at me and kissed me as if I was a tiresome child and I panic at the sound of his name!

A depressing conviction formed in her mind that she was far too vulnerable to physical male attraction. First Patrick and now this dark stranger who must have forgotten her existence by now. But I didn't go all the way with Patrick, she consoled herself. She'd enjoyed his company until he tried to force the pace, taking it for granted that she would give in eventually as the obvious extension to their friendship and professional contacts.

Did I ever truly love him? Did I ever really feel that life without him would be a desert? she wondered. She glanced at the distant sandhills. Life would be a desert without love, but she had yet to find the elusive emotion that could last. She smiled a little sadly. One man called Patrick and one called Jean-Louis, both totally different, but both with the threatening sexuality that made her back away, however much she felt attracted. One man with fair hair and blue eyes and the other dark. The flying wheels gripped the runway with a squeal at last. In Tunis, the spell would fade and he would be just another man in the sun if she met him again. She thrust aside the memory of a pale grey silk shirt against her arm and taut breast.

Angela reached for one of the flight bags, but Vassila put a restraining hand on her arm. 'They will come,' she said, and two men came from the back of the small jet plane and saluted before taking the luggage. Madame followed them and Angela came behind with Aysha, who was carried by a huge man with a terrifying moustache who looked as if he might be a fugitive from a band of brigands. There were advantages in being with a diplomatic group, Angela decided. A line of tourists from a charter plane moved slowly towards Customs, while the family group were shown to a long black limousine a few yards from the private plane.

The Tunis air was hot and dry; the jacket that had seemed cool in London now seemed suffocating, and Angela removed it. Aysha sat close, her head on the bare arm and a contented smile on her face.

'Will the medical equipment be sent on soon?' Angela asked anxiously, glancing back at the airport.

'It will be in the next car,' said Vassila, not bothering to check. 'I pine to visit London and Paris, and yet when I come back over the desert my heart leaps home.' She laughed. 'To you this is a muddle of flat roofs and bare ground, sand and desolation.' Angela shook her head. 'It is polite to deny it, but it is so.' The dark eyes were serious. 'I promise you that when you have smelled the parched earth and run the sand of the desert through your fingers you may go away, but you will return. Tunisia can be a drug to many whose roots are not in the sand but who come as you do, as a friend.'

'I thought you lived in Tunis?' Angela looked out at the rough patches of vegetation that flanked the white road and the high hedges of cactus that made surreal shapes against the vivid blue sky.

'We have an apartment there for when I visit or go shopping and if my husband needs me for receptions there, but we live in Sidi Bou Said, where the air is clear and the breeze is often cool from the sea. Sidi is close to Carthage and many of the old Roman settlements, and further on is La Marsa where the last Bey of Tunis lived in his summer palace with all his wives and concubines and the eunuchs of his harem.' Madame smiled. 'That tale is for the tourists who love to hear the salacious details, but since Habib Bourguiba came to power a more puritanical era began, and much has changed in our country. Now it changes again.' Her face tightened with the memory of the attempt on her husband's life. 'But violence is still not as common in our country as it is in many.'

'I know so little about Tunisia,' Angela confessed. 'My half-brother writes few details, and I have only second-hand reports of the country.'

'Ah, yes, you have a brother here. Does he know of your visit?'

'No. I have his address, but I was scared to attempt the phone as I might be confronted with a flow of fast Arabic!'

'When we have eaten and Aysha has been settled, you will use the telephone after my secretary has contacted your brother for you,' Madame told her.

Angela smiled with a tinge of disbelief. 'This is all ridiculous! You are so kind, and there's really no need for Aysha to have me with her. There'll be no lasting trace of scarring, and I was told that the slight strabismus will not be treated yet except by exercises. Anything needed can be done by an efficient and intelligent employee.'

'That is not the message I received,' Vassila said blandly. 'And Aysha has taken to you and trusts you.'

It was too bad of the agency to agree to this assignment, thought Angela. They must have done it to make sure of the fat fee her stay in Tunisia would bring them, way above her own generous pay. Hospitals grumbled over staff shortages, and here she was in luxury and near-idleness in a wonderful climate. She could think of at least two surgeons who would scream for her services if she was available. 'I'm very happy to be here,' she said, 'but it's only fair to say that you're wasting money by having me here.'

'How can one put a price on peace of mind?' asked Vassila quietly. 'You comforted us when my child was injured and I was frightened and tired.' She made a curiously deferential movement with her hands. 'You are my sister. You are welcome to our house, and what we have is yours.' It was an echo of the past, the hospitality of the desert. 'My sister, you must call me Vassila.'

The car stopped in a grove of orange trees that cast a dense shade in the afternoon sun. In the distance was a lawn as green as any in England, and the tall blue-painted gates of wrought iron closed behind the limousine as they drove on to a single-storeyed house sprawled on the side of a slope, partly on columns that left an area of deep shade under the main structure. Moorish windows looked out on to bright flowers and exotic succulent plants in earthenware pots on ledges of rough sandstone. The view over the valley was of green trees beyond which were houses tumbled together along the sides of narrow streets. Faintly, Angela heard the sound of music, repetitive and compelling, sensual and hypnotic, the sound of Tunisia. It sent a cool tremor through her body as if someone had held aside a bead curtain to show her something of which she had yet to dream.

Aysha was hot and tired, and it was over an hour later when Angela was free to go to her room to change. The child sat up in bed in a clean cotton nightdress, after the injured eye had been irrigated with the sterile saline solution that had come with the medical equipment. Albucid drops made sure that the healing process would continue, and a fresh eye-pad gave protection from infection or further injury.

'She will sleep now,' Vassila said with satisfaction when she came to kiss her daughter goodnight. 'Have you everything you need, Angela?'

'Could I have a supply of water that's been boiled for at least twenty minutes and allowed to cool in a sealed container?' Angela requested. 'I need quite a lot for irrigations, and it must be pure.'

'I don't need to sleep, Maman. I am not tired, and you promised that *mon oncle* would come to see me,' pleaded Aysha.

'If he comes and finds you awake, he will be very cross with me and with Angela.'

Angela turned to leave them together and to go to her room. If Dr Joudet came now, he would find a hot and sticky female with damp hair clinging in tendrils round her face and a very shiny nose, but Vassila clapped her hands and a girl appeared wearing a light robe such as the locals wore. She gave a wide smile and motioned to Angela to follow her.

The room was elegant and cool and the air was redolent of orange blossom. Angela showered and finished under an icy tingle of sharp cold spray. She drank from the jug of iced fresh orange juice on the marble table and put on a simple cotton dress of palest green, that hung in folds over her hips and floated behind her as she walked, lifting and clinging against her thighs in an artless flow. Her high-heeled sandals were no more than bands of silver and black to match the slender belt on the dress, and the tight bodice was decorated with tiny black buttons from low neck to waist.

She caught her hair up on one side in a wide comb of antique design given to her by her grandmother, and wondered if the effect was slightly provocative, but shrugged and applied a touch of soft red lipstick and a dusting of grey-green eye-shadow to give her confidence.

Suddenly uncertain, she paused and took a deep breath before following the girl along a marble-floored corridor. She wondered if she should have dressed more formally, and was relieved to see that

Vassila had changed into a slim silk shift that clung to her curves with all the expert simplicity of a Paris couturier.

Vassila introduced her to the four guests as 'a friend from England,' and no mention was made of the reason for her being there. 'Yes, Aysha is well but tired and resting, and Ali, my husband, is busy in Tunis on business,' she added. It was clear that the ben Ksars were determined to keep a low profile on the events of the past week.

Wine was served in fine goblets to those who drank wine, but two of the guests were more orthodox and drank only fruit juices. The food was varied and very French, followed by the traditional sweetmeats of Tunisia, with huge bowls of fresh fruit, but of Dr Joudet there was no sign, and Angela wondered how a Frenchman could make this country his home when he had access to all the sophistication of modern surgery in London or Paris.

Vassila glanced at the gold watch on her wrist. 'If you would like to telephone now, I will ask Mohammed to get through to the mining office, then we can have coffee on the terrace.'

Angela found herself in a very businesslike office with a telex and an array of telephones and computers. Mohammed was quiet and efficient and seemed to be in no hurry to go off duty, as if he was on call for Madame's wishes at all hours. The line was bad, but at last through static, voices came clearly, and Mohammed turned and smiled, holding out the receiver to her.

'*Dermot*? You'll never guess where I am!' said Angela excitedly.

'Angie? It can't be! This call must cost a fortune from the UK. Is something wrong?'

'No, I'm here in Tunis, or somewhere near. I'm here on a case, and when it's over I can see you.' She heard voices outside the office door, a man asking if he could use the phone and Mohammed explaining. She listened to Dermot trying to think of ways to get closer to her, but she could tell from his tone that work was heavy and urgent and this might be difficult.

'I just can't get to Tunis this week,' he told her.

'I can come to you. Is there somewhere where I can stay?'

'Only my bungalow, which is very basic, but there's a hotel a few miles away where visiting bigwigs stay, if you can afford that. I can help out, but how to get you here?'

'It's wonderful to hear your voice. I've missed you so much.' Angela paused. 'I can't make any definite plans today, but I'll be in touch as soon as I'm free. You'd love my little patient, and the family are marvellous. Yes, I'll be in touch soon. Good-night, darling. I can't wait to see you.'

She turned away, her face aglow with pleasure. The same old Dermot, vague but delighted to hear from her, even when his attention was half down that awful mine. She gave a self-indulgent giggle. I'm so lucky to have him, even if he is a bit mad, she thought—then gasped as she recognised the man who lounged up against the door. Jean-Louis

Joudet smiled enigmatically as if only half pleased
to see her. He extended his hand in formal greeting
and she saw, with a sense of shock, that his eyes
were not brown as she had thought but the dark
blue of Parma violets that look almost black in a
half light.

The touch of his hand was cool and light and the
contact brief, but those eyes burned into hers as if
trying to read her heart, coldly assessing what he
saw.

She wanted to cry out her sense of loss, of the
ebbing of warmth and the end of something that
had hardly begun.

'Have you quite finished on the phone?' he asked.

'Yes. It was a bad line, but we managed.' She
gave an embarrassed laugh. 'I can't recall a time
when ringing my brother wasn't difficult. He's in
mining, and works in very out-of-the-way places.'
Why don't I shut up? she thought. He doesn't want
to hear me rabbiting on about my brother. I'm just
a girl who kept him waiting for the telephone. He's
anxious to make this call, she decided. A bit late for
business, so it could be to a woman.

The dark eyes glinted with humour and a sudden
flash of something that took away the sombre for-
mality. 'Mines are notoriously bad for telephones,'
he agreed gravely.

Angela walked back to Vassila, hoping she
wouldn't stumble on her high heels as she walked
away from the man who continued to stare after
her. She fumed inwardly. He's laughing at me again!
I either make him resent me as I did when I was on

the phone or he finds me comic! Just as well, as she could now forget the first brief chemistry that had passed between them in London.

A huge coffee-tray rested on a low table and small dishes of various sweetmeats were arranged among sprays of orange blossom and jasmine and dark green leaves. Angela sank on to a soft reclining chair, and lights on the roof attracted moths and other insects away from the people drinking coffee. Music and laughter from a distant café came softly through the night, making a friendly background to the darkness.

Dr Jean-Louis Joudet came and sat on a vacant chair on the far side of the table, facing her. His long legs stretched under the table and he accepted coffee with a smile. His eyes and mobile mouth showed relaxed contentment, and Angela wondered what the woman was like who had made this transformation from the air of cool rejection that she had sensed when he saw her.

She looked away into the soft darkness beyond the trees to the shadow of a tall minaret jabbing at the stars. Her hair drooped across her face and she hid behind its veil, knowing that she was under the scrutiny of those dark blue eyes. Must he stare at her when he was probably far away in his thoughts?

Vassila sat by his side. 'Did you get through?' she asked.

'Yes, immediately,' he told her. 'I have to go to Sousse soon, but I may come back to see Aysha tomorrow and again in three days' time.'

Angela looked up sharply. If he wasn't coming to

examine Aysha again for three days she would not
be able to leave the ben Ksar household and see her
brother. It was annoying when there was no real
need for her to be there after tomorrow.

'You will fly?' Vassila smiled. 'I suppose you will
spend all your time in that charity clinic and forget
to bring me my spices!'

In the shadow, Angela felt forgotten, but she was
fascinated by the two beautiful people laughing
together and completely at ease in a warm familiar
way. I'm a stranger here who will be forgotten five
minutes after I leave their full lives, she decided.
She took another honey cake and nibbled it, and
knew why so many middle-aged Arab women put
on weight. Coffee and sweetmeats and little exercise
must play havoc with a good figure. Well, I shan't
be here for long enough to suffer that fate, she
thought, but the idea of leaving was becoming less
and less attractive.

'She must stay away from the sun's glare for a
while and then I must look at her squint again,' she
heard Dr Joudet say. 'It's no good looking at me
with those great big pleading eyes, Vassila. You
know it should have been treated years ago, before
I was able to help you, and Ali agrees with me.' He
put up a hand when Vassila began to protest.
'Would you rather wait until you go to London
again, or do you want me to perform what is really
a very simple operation here?'

'Not London. . .yet.' She glanced at the other
guests, who were leaving after many goodbyes, and
couldn't add, Not after the attempt on my husband.

The three of them were alone again. 'It must be done,' he said. The force of his personality came through the polite and gentle tones, and Angela knew that he could demand respect and gain what he wanted just by the firm inflexion of his voice and the piercing magnetism of his dark eyes. She shivered. This was a man who knew what he wanted and took it. She saw again the beautifully moulded mouth and knew that he could give even more than he demanded, of passion and desire. 'What is the alternative?' he asked gently.

Vassila cast an agonised glance towards Angela, then blushed deeply. 'Oh, what must you think of me? I am a bad hostess. I forget! I am with people I like and I take it that they know each other. I was forgetting that you have not really met. Angela, I would like you to meet our dear friend Jean-Louis Joudet, who cured my darling Aysha. Jean-Louis, may I present Angela, who is becoming dear to us all.'

Dr Joudet rose from his seat and walked slowly round the table to take Angela by the hand, his eyes inscrutable as he gazed down at her. She felt at a disadvantage and wondered if she should have struggled to her feet from the low chair during the introduction.

'Sister. . . Angela,' he said. 'I am delighted to make your acquaintance.'

'Dr Joudet,' she replied with a tight smile. He was teasing again, pretending that he had never spoken to her and certainly had never kissed her, and from his manner he wanted Vassila to know that he would take only a professional interest in the nursing sister from the agency.

He smiled as if he had just conceived a very bright idea. 'This meeting is very convenient. If Sister Angela is looking after Aysha, she can help me with the strabismus operation and nurse her until she is better.'

'Of course!' Vassila clapped her hands together. 'If Angela is here, I shall be happy to let you operate. You will stay?' she asked.

'I don't know.' Angela was confused. 'The agency might send for me.'

'The agency will have you back when I have finished with you and not before. Leave it to me, Sister.' Angela's lips twitched into a reluctant smile of admiration. The head of the agency and Miss Pritchard would be no match for this man. But no one had asked her what she wanted to do!

Again, the conversation was over her head. 'We mustn't be selfish, Louis,' said Vassila. 'Angela must have time first to meet her brother before she can be expected to stay with Aysha for several days without a break.' Dr Joudet sipped his coffee and listened politely as if he knew nothing of the girl sitting in half shadow, with the blonde wonder of her hair tumbling past one eyebrow. 'Angela has a brother who is a mining engineer,' Vassila continued. 'He is working as an advisor at the phosphate mine but is now visiting Bizerta to take part in a trade delegation. Isn't that so, Angela?'

'I was hoping to meet him in Bizerta as the mine

is so far away and he isn't keen for me to go there,'
Angela explained.

'It would be too primitive for a woman travelling
alone,' the doctor remarked.

'I'm not afraid of travelling alone. I've been all
over Europe and the States.'

Vassila and the doctor exchanged amused and
indulgent glances. 'This is Africa,' he said. 'Women
are seldom seen alone, either travelling or in hotels.'

'How old-fashioned!' said Angela with a hint of
irritation.

'We care for our women here,' he replied.

'But you are French, and surely the French are
one of the most liberated countries in the world.
You can't have that archaic opinion!'

'It depends on the woman,' he said calmly. 'And
I consider myself to be Tunisian.'

'Because you live here it doesn't mean you have
to accept all the customs of the country,' Angela
retorted. 'Western women go as they please, usually
in perfect safety. In any case, since Bourguiba came
to power, hasn't the position of women changed
here? Even after he was deposed, liberation went
on.'

'In theory, yes,' he said with a maddening smile.
'But look around and you'll see few women in the
cafés, either alone or with men.' His cool arrogance
was annoying.

'Are you telling me I must wait here for my
brother to visit me as I can't travel alone?' she
demanded.

'Not at all. Vassila will put a car at your disposal

while you are here, and you can be driven anywhere you wish.'

'But I can't catch a bus or go on a train alone? Have coffee in a village or walk alone in Tunis?' Her eyes blazed and her cheeks were pink with annoyance.

'Tunis is different. It is like any other modern town, full of tourists and liberated ladies. Go there as much as you wish, and to the modern hotel complexes.'

'Thank you,' Angela said wryly. 'I was beginning to think I should wear a veil.'

'Not a veil, but you would look charming in a *haik*.' Her eyelids fluttered before his intent gaze and she caught her breath. 'But I have a better and more practical idea,' he said in a voice that showed he had made up his mind that she would agree. 'I will fly you to Bizerta and show you a typical Tunisian village.'

'I couldn't possibly ask you to waste your time on. . .a complete stranger,' she said, and had the satisfaction of seeing him incline his head and give an ironic smile.

'But I feel that we do know each other, Sister,' he said smoothly. 'I am not being generous. I shall expect something in return.' Her heart beat faster, but she could read nothing in the hooded eyes as he bent forward to put his coffee cup on the tray. 'I want you to come with me to the clinic in Sousse and help me for a morning.'

'This idea has only just occurred to you?' Angela seethed with anger, but only her eyes gave her away. A phone call telling the agency that she was needed for Aysha assured him of a nursing sister to use in his own clinic! It explained everything. The agency refused to send nurses abroad to work in places where they might pick up more infection than they cured, and only wealthy families like the ben Ksars qualified for the skill of people like Angela, unless they went with charitable organisations or VSO.

A string of objections flashed through her mind, but she merely set her chin at a defiant angle and glared. 'I suppose it's a fair exchange,' she admitted. 'If you don't find me a liability, as I speak no Arabic and have little or no idea of what makes the average Tunisian ill or how they live.'

'They are human beings who need help,' he said quietly, and she blushed, sensing that she had sounded patronising.

'I must go and see if Aysha is asleep,' said Vassila. 'No, there is no need for you to come, Angela. Stay with Louis and become friends.'

'Alas, I have to leave now,' he said. 'I shall come to see Aysha at ten tomorrow, and drive you to the airstrip so that we can be in Bizerta for lunch with your brother.'

'But how will he know I'm on my way?' Angela asked anxiously.

'He knows. It is all arranged.' Jean-Louis Joudet smiled and stepped forward to kiss Vassila lightly on both cheeks, then kissed her hand. He turned to Angela and took her hand. Pulling her towards him, he kissed her in like manner and looked down into

the wide green eyes. It was only the French saluta-
tion that had no meaning other than polite greeting
or farewell, but she trembled as his hand closed
firmly on hers for a second or two longer than
necessary.

He had arranged everything as he wanted it. In
his eyes, she read the expression she had seen in the
eyes of a gambler who had been successful, a mere
glimmer of laughing triumph. She wondered if he
ever failed to get what he wanted.

CHAPTER THREE

THE unreality of it all made Angela laugh, and the man at her side, piloting the small executive jet, glanced sideways before resuming his forward gaze along the dry airstrip between the lines of oil drums and crude lighting. Men in flowing robes dragged the chocks clear of the wheels, and the slipstream made the loose garments eddy like tossed waste paper as the plane gained height. Turbanned dark faces smiled, and rapid loud Arabic faded. The heat of the sun drying the last of the winter rains and bringing colour back to the sand made a picture that she knew she would never forget.

'I can't believe I'm here,' she explained, to justify her sudden laughter. 'It's ridiculous. I should be back in the clinic in London, rubbing surgical spirit on Shane Winsconsin's pressure points or teaching Mr Macintosh the rudiments of his high-fibre diet, while the wind blows cold through London.'

'Don't tell me you're homesick already?' The trees by the house where Angela had spent the night were now a splash of green on an ochre landscape. Behind them white houses became flat white stones in the desert, and as they rose with the sun behind them, the sandhills lay bleakly below and the sea glinted silver and blue at the edge of what must be the biggest beach on earth, the Sahara.

'It's wonderful!' she breathed. If this was a high, then she was on cloud nine.

'By all means become interested and amused by my country, but please don't laugh at us.' Dr Joudet was smiling and seemed relaxed and even better-looking in the strong morning light. As he concentrated on the controls, Angela had time to observe him. His skin was smooth and light brown in a way that seemed permanent, unlike the suntan of men on a brief holiday, or even one working in a sunny country. His dark hair was almost black and his nose was straight and aquiline. His name was French and his eyes were dark blue, but there was something more. She saw the slender strength of his long fingers and was disturbed by the soft trace of hair on the backs of his hands.

'Why do you identify so closely with Tunisia?' she asked.

He banked slightly and she saw the range of hills away to the west on which a line of camels made slow progress, leaving a curving track of ruffled sand. It was too far away to see the colour of the camel blankets, but she could imagine the same line of camels plodding the same course centuries ago. 'I am Tunisian,' he told her. 'I live here and work here, and my family is here.'

'I see.' A leaden sensation robbed her of the bubbling happiness she had felt as soon as she sat by his side in the plane. What a fool she was to imagine he wanted to be with her because. . .just because. A family was a wife and children and perhaps a mother and father, but she couldn't ask him anything of a more personal nature.

'My father was French and lived here, taking a leading part in the transition from French influence to full Tunisian freedom,' he added.

'He's dead?'

'Yes. My mother lives in Tunis and has a house at Sfax in the south, and I have a sister too.'

Angela waited for a minute for him to tell her that he was married, but had to speak to break the tension between them. 'Just a sister? I have only a half-brother, but no parents. His name is Dermot.'

'I know. This is a strange situation full of coincidences. I had already met your brother.'

'You've met him?' She turned a glowing face towards him. 'When was this?'

'My sister is in love with an engineer, a German who works with your brother. I went to the mine with her some time ago and met them there, and this arrangement is very welcome as I wanted to see Karl again.'

'I believe you had everything planned!' laughed Angela.

'I asked Mohammed to get in touch with Karl and he said that you had been talking on that line. I spoke to Karl and arranged that he should bring Dermot to have lunch with us as I was bringing you with me.'

'What about your sister? Will she be there?'

His face hardened. 'She is unable to come. My mother has other plans for her today. She must visit the mosque at Kairoum.'

'What a shame! It would have been quite a party,' said Angela.

'Quite a party,' he agreed, but once again she felt excluded from his thoughts and settled back to look at the changeless desert below them.

It came as no surprise now to be whisked away from the airport in a huge yellow car that was waiting for them by arrangement. The driver wore the familiar scarlet *chechia*, commonly called a fez after the Turkish influence. His colourful *djellaba* was spotless, and he spoke in clipped French instead of the expected Arabic. In a few minutes, the car stopped at a waterfront restaurant away from the industrial environment of the busy docks, where the tramp steamers and tankers took away exports of olive oil and dates, oranges and phosphates, and brought the life blood of commerce of Tunisia. The sea was blue and unpolluted, but the hotel guests seemed to prefer swimming in the huge pool by the beach.

Angela went to the rest-room and found everything as clean and pretty as any she had used in London hotels. Tunisian music played softly, and she emerged fresh and eager to meet her brother.

'Angie!' She was swept up into a bear-hug. 'It's so good to see you!' She smoothed down her crumpled cream skirt and tweaked the cotton shirt back inside the waistband, laughing at his impetuous onslaught.

'You don't change!' she told him. 'I need to wear a jumpsuit when you say hello!'

He viewed the bright pink shirt with approval. 'You look like a strawberry ice,' he remarked.

'Slightly melted,' she replied, 'But it's heavenly to be here.'

Air-conditioning made the hotel cool, and she was curious to be introduced to the man in love with Dr Joudet's sister. It was easy to imagine a pretty French girl after meeting the brother, but the two men stood by the window and seemed ill at ease. Perhaps Dr Joudet was doing a 'big brother' act and disapproved of any relationship that Karl wanted with his sister, she thought.

'Is that Karl?' she asked. 'I thought they knew each other well, but they look very tense,' she added.

Dermot took her arm. 'Let's have a drink—they're busy. I'll introduce you later after we've exchanged all our news.' They sat by a low table flanked by settees of deep cushions. 'You'll find the orange juice good. It's the most refreshing drink here. It's always freshly squeezed and icy cold, and I only drink alcohol in the evenings when the air is cooler. I find I drink less alcohol here.' He ordered drinks for the other two men, knowing that they would have the same. 'It's also diplomatic to have soft drinks during the day when I'm with orthodox Muslims. It becomes a good habit.'

Six men sat at a table drinking tea or orange juice and talking loudly. They ignored Angela, but she knew that when she entered the room there had been silence and they remained aware of here. It made her glad she had worn a shirt with long sleeves

and her skirt came well below the knees, not to
offend the orthodox Tunisians she might meet away
from the more sophisticated places.

Dermot smiled at several people coming and
going and spoke to a pretty dark girl carrying a
briefcase and folder of papers. 'She's a secretary
with the American consortium that I'm here to
meet,' he told Angela. 'A lot of the girls now work
and don't wear the veil. Many train as doctors and
nurses. Most of them are dark-haired, and you, my
love, are a bit conspicuous with all that blonde hair.
Don't walk down any dark alleys at night,' he
added, laughing.

'That's silly! Every man I've met so far has been
far more correct than the guys at home,' Angela
assured him.

'That's because you're under the wing of a very
influential family, and word gets around. I don't
suppose you made a modest entrance to Bizerta
today? That plane is the envy of every businessman
without air transport. I wish I could afford one.'

'Does it belong to the ben Ksars?' she asked.

'No, it's Joudet's. He's from a very well-loaded
Tunisian family.'

'You say Tunisian, but he's French,' she said. 'Do
they have to swear allegiance to live here?'

Dermot looked at her curiously. 'Nothing like
that, but his family have been here for a long time.'
He sipped his juice and didn't look at her directly.
'How did you meet him? Why is he sufficiently
interested in you to bring you here today?'

Angela laughed. 'Stop looking like a po-faced

maiden aunt! He's not a pick-up! I know that "sliding away" expression. You always put it on when you think I've done something of which you'd disapprove.' She told him how she had come to nurse Aysha and the sudden decision to come home with the family. 'She may have a small operation, so this will be my only chance of leaving her for a while. Dr Joudet was coming here to see Karl and it all slotted in together.'

'I see. It's only a professional arrangement.' His face cleared.

'Dermot! I'm a big girl now. I'm not just your nasty, naughty little sister. I could look after myself even if pursued by a handsome sheikh on a white horse. Believe me, there's more danger in a shut-away room in a private hospital than I've encountered here.'

'I hope you're right,' he said shortly. 'Here's Karl. I think they're ready to eat. Louis has gone to the restaurant and he's beckoning.' He made the introduction to Karl, and Angela found her hand taken briefly by a serious-looking blond boy with a densely freckled face and bright blue eyes. He, at least, of all the men she had met in Tunisia would be safe, she decided. He looked kind and his handshake was warm, and she thought Dr Joudet's sister would be safe with him.

They sat below the sweeping fronds of a palm tree on a shaded terrace through which a gentle breeze from the sea dispelled the worst of the heat, and ate iced soup and a dish of chicken and almonds followed by fresh fruit and the inevitable sweet dishes. It was wonderful to sit by the man who had a link with her brother and whose voice made her want to smile and hope he would smile at her.

She tried to forget that he had a family and could have no place for her in his life. She listened to the talk between the men, and when there was a lull in the conversation she asked if Dr Joudet would be returning to England or France soon.

He looked surprised, as if Europe was far away and even further from his thoughts. Angela stirred uneasily. Did this country have that sort of magic that a man forgot his roots? She recalled the words that Vassila had used. 'Once you have smelled the parched earth and run the sands of the desert through your fingers. . .' It couldn't be true about the doctor. This was just a part of his work, and his appearance in Sidi Bou Said had nothing to do with magic or the fact that a blonde nursing sister would be there.

Among the fair heads at the table, Dr Joudet looked almost as dark as the Arabs at the next table. 'Do those men come from Bizerta?' she asked Karl.

'No, they are from the south. We know them through the consortium, and we find they are hard businessmen,' he added with an admiring smile. 'After centuries of the desert with all its hardships and the rigours of a nomadic life, they still keep a fierce independence and a healthy suspicion of other men doing business with them. But they keep a bargain.' He looked about the room. 'It's not easy to know who is Tunisian and who isn't. Look over there.'

'You mean the girl in the dark blue dress talking to the man in the grey suit?' Angela thought the girl looked like an older version of Aysha.

'The girl is obviously Tunisian, but the man is of mixed cultures. This country has been invaded by everyone, from the Phoenicians, the Greeks, the Turks, to the French, and you see traces of these in the faces of many you meet. One man may wear *djellabas* and speak nothing but Arabic, even though he may have a French face, and others who are quite different speak French and English and are very European, and yet are dark and Arabic. It's a fascinating mixture, and it makes for an interesting race of people.'

'The man certainly looks like a French or German businessman,' Angela remarked.

'I hope to marry a Tunisian, and take her back to Germany after I finish this job,' said Karl.

Angela glanced at Dr Joudet and wondered if Karl had told him that he had another girlfriend apart from his sister, then the conversation became more general and at last the group at the next table gathered up papers and briefcases and left the restaurant. 'I must go too,' said Dermot. 'We have a big meeting and Karl and I have to be there.' He kissed Angela lightly on the cheek. 'I hope we can arrange something before you go home,' he said.

'There's no hurry,' said Dr Joudet. 'I have work for your sister to do and she will be here for some time.'

'I have to report back to the agency soon,' she pointed out. 'My contract for six weeks makes it plain that I have to work out the terms of agreement wherever they send me if a case finishes sooner than expected.'

'If you choose to leave when Aysha is completely well, then you must leave,' he said, regarding her with sombre eyes, but she sensed that he had no intention of letting her go before he gave her permission. She waved to her brother as he went through the foyer and found herself alone with the doctor.

The restaurant was suddenly empty and quiet. 'Has everyone gone back to work?' she asked.

He smiled lazily, and shrugged. 'You see, business calls, and two lonely people are left to amuse each other.'

'I'm sure you're busy too,' she replied nervously. 'Shouldn't we get back to Aysha?'

'And make the men at the airstrip work in this blinding heat?' He shook his head as if amused. 'What can we do this afternoon until the heat is less? If you were in Sidi you would rest during the afternoon, and if you would like that, I can arrange a room here for you.' His gaze travelled over her face and body, and suddenly she wanted to pull a protective shawl round her, or as the Tunisian women did, draw the folds of a soft *haik* to cover her face as if she was afraid to allow a man to gaze at her.

I must be going crazy! she thought resentfully. At home, I take it for granted that men look at me. It's a compliment to be thought desirable. But here, I know that there's passion behind that smooth admiration and something more savage than I've ever encountered, something more relentless than I can handle.

She forced a smile. 'I'm not tired,' she said. 'If I tried to sleep I'd be restless, and I'd rather look at the town.' If he had any bright ideas about sharing her siesta, this was the moment to make it clear that she wasn't an easy lay!

His mocking smile said, 'Coward', but the words came only as, 'A pity. You'll find it hot in the desert.'

'There's plenty of shade in the town,' Angela persisted, trying to control her uneven breathing. Why had one mocking smile and a glance from under slumbrous eyelids brought back the emotion that had engulfed her at their first meeting? This time they had not even touched, but the warm air was charged with a magnetic current that threatened to pull them together and destroy her sanity.

'I'll see if the car is available,' he said. 'I promised to show you a typical village, so if you are quite ready we'll go.'

Angela fetched her bag and the floppy linen hat she had brought with her, and under its brim and behind huge dark glasses, she felt safer and able to confront the intense eyes that made her feel weak and unprotected.

'It will be cooler in the car,' Dr Joudet said. She looked round for the driver. 'I shall drive. We are more at ease without a chauffeur,' he added.

You may be, she thought drily. Dermot—help!

He handed her into her seat, and his touch was warm and caressing. He picked up a fold of her skirt and placed it carefully inside the car before closing the door. It was a gesture of polite concern, but the slim brown fingers seemed to take their time over it, savouring the experience as if he caressed her bare leg and left a lingering touch on the smooth skin.

The air-conditioning was comfortable, and she relaxed as Dr Joudet avoided potholes in the dusty road. 'Thank you for bringing me to see Dermot,' she said. 'We haven't met for over a year, and I must make an effort to see that it isn't as long again.'

'That can be arranged,' he replied. 'You must stay long enough to get to know us well. We are proud of our country and we like to share it, but we don't want too many tourists. We do want and need friends, however.'

'What of France? Doesn't France demand the same loyalty?'

'I am Tunisian by birth. My mother was in Tunis when I was born and my father took Tunisian nationality to ensure her inheritance. She, as you have probably guessed, is a Berber. I am of mixed race but essentially Tunisian.'

'Of course!' Angela laughed. 'I think of you as French, and then suddenly you look like the men who sat at the next table today.' Her eyes widened. 'And your sister? Is she like you?'

'She is more Berber than French, and my mother tries to keep her like that. When my father died, my sister Yasmin was made to take the Muslim faith, although my father had willed that we should choose which religious path we wished to follow, if any. She dresses as a Berber woman and goes to the mosque, but she is in love with Karl and I think will soon become Westernised.'

'Does your mother dress as an Arab lady or like Vassila?'

'She goes to Paris and buys smart clothes and is very beautiful, then she comes here and changes into the clothes of her race. . .when it suits her to do so.' His voice was bitter. 'At present, she is the perfect Berber lady intent on making her daughter obey Islam, and she hopes to marry her to a wealthy businessman.' He accelerated as a small village came into view. 'Perhaps it would be better if she did and gave up Karl,' he added quietly.

'Oh, no! If she's really in love, surely she would be very unhappy in a forced marriage?'

He laughed, and once more his tone was light and mocking. 'Who would have thought that there was such sentiment under that cool smooth hair? Do you think that love conquers all?'

Angela was glad the dark glasses hid her eyes. 'I don't know. I'm not the girl in love,' she said. 'How can I judge her feelings?'

'The combination of French and Arab makes a passionate mix,' he said. His eyes were wicked with humour as if he knew that she was reacting to his charisma.

What had seemed a village spread into a small town as they drew closer, and he parked in the shade by a side turning off the main street. Out in the open, the heat was oppressive, and Angela wondered if she would regret the expedition. Open-fronted shops selling pottery and carpets cast the only shade as they walked slowly along the length of the street. Men sat on rugs in the shade, making little effort to advertise their wares, and a sleepy atmosphere prevailed, broken by the bleating of sheep tethered outside the butcher's shop.

'It's almost real!' Angela stared at a ceramic cockerel, huge and resplendent in sculptured feathers of every shade, ready to herald the dawn of a day, or of a new life.

'I must take you to Nabeul or Hammamet where whole families work on these.' Dr Joudet touched the crimson comb gently.

'"And as the cock crew, those who stood before
The tavern shouted. . .open then the door!
You know how little time we have to stay,
And once departed may return, no more."' He smiled briefly, but his eyes were sad.

'I've been recalling lines from Omar since I came here. It's everywhere,' Angela said in a low voice, and shivered. 'The desert we passed through seems so permanent, as if it will swallow everything up in time.'

He caught her hand and raised it to his lips. 'How little time we have to stay, Angela.' He released her and she kept her lips from trembling, and knew that he couldn't read her eyes. Was this the subtle approach of a man who wanted her and was ruthless enough to use every weapon in his charming, rich and intelligent armoury? She tried to think of Patrick, the man she had imagined could break her heart, but she could recall nothing. Other men had tried to make love to her and she had avoided the issue, keeping them as friends, but this man would expect all or nothing from a woman he desired. Her panic grew. If he tries to make love to me, I'm lost! she thought. But if I turn away, he'll vanish as a mirage fades and I shall never see him again.

'Is this what we came to see? China birds?' she said in a effort to sound detached.

'No, but it is a part of the town.' She followed him to a white building with a row of windows along its length and he pushed open the door as if he belonged there. A white-robed man bowed slightly and made the graceful gesture of hand from waist to chin as if offering hospitality. The two men spoke in Arabic, then the man went quickly up a spiral staircase of wrought iron, and Angela looked about her with curiosity.

'It's a dispensary!' she said.

'People come here with minor ailments and injuries and are treated by orderlies and lay staff, unless they are severely hurt or ill, and then they are taken to Sousse where we have a good clinic and surgery,' the doctor told her.

'Is that where you expect me to help you?' She took a deep breath. 'Dr Joudet, I don't know what you expect, but I speak no Arabic and have no knowledge of the routine of medicine in this country.'

He was examining a ledger, but left it open and

leaned on the desk. 'I do have a name,' he suggested mildly, completely ignoring her remarks. 'Would it tax your ingenuity to call me Jean-Louis, or Louis if you prefer? I think you would find that more natural than my other name, Husain.' He turned another page and his face darkened.

He was angry, with a savage twist to his mouth, but Angela knew instinctively that the anger was not for her. He picked up the ledger again and slammed it on to the desk as the man returned, talking volubly and making many excuses. Reluctantly, he held out a sheaf of papers, which the doctor examined quickly, his anger mounting. He spoke at length to the now cringing man.

'What's wrong?' Angela asked.

'This fool needs his head examined! I saw a case here a week ago that needed further care and told him to arrange transport to Sousse. He now says that as the man didn't come back to the clinic he assumed he was either better or dead.' He made a note in a book and threw down the folder. 'We'll have to take a look, but God knows what we shall find.'

He spoke again, and the man scurried to various shelves for painkillers, antibiotics and dressings. He packed them into a case and stood back as the two unwelcome visitors made for the door, but followed them, shouting instructions as to where they would find the patient.

It was difficult to run in high heels and almost impossible to breathe in the intense heat. 'Wait for me!' Angela cried, but Louis was too angry to hear her and strode on, leaving her to follow him. When she turned the corner he was disappearing into a small house.

She hesitated by the paved patio until his head appeared round the edge of the wall. 'Well, come in if you're coming,' he ordered.

The room was lavishly decorated with embroidered cushions and lace and the simple furniture was light and durable. A woman with an anxious face sat by the window as if she heard nothing, and a low groan from the one bedroom brought the doctor and the nursing sister to the door. A man lay on the bed, looking very thin and ill. He turned from side to side as if to drag himself away from his pain, and his eyes were fever-bright. One leg lay on top of the sheet which covered the rest of his body, and Angela saw a dark swelling in the thigh muscle.

'What is it?' she asked.

'He came to the clinic for a dressing and said it was only a scratch he had got when he was with his camels. I didn't see it at the time as he had left the village again, but I suspected that he might have a bullet in there, from what the orderly said.'

'A bullet!' Angela stared in horror.

'He wouldn't go to Sousse, as he was afraid of being arrested for stealing camels. There have been many camel thefts around here and the Bedouin traders are a bit trigger-happy. One camel in his string was found to have another man's mark on it, although he swore he had bought it from him, but a bullet in the thigh takes a bit of explaining,' Louis said bluntly.

'We can't leave him here! How do we get him to Tunis or Sousse?'

'Sousse would be best as his wife has relatives there who could visit him. She is worse than useless. When these people lose hope, they sit and piously say it is the will of Allah.'

By this time, the medical orderly had arrived with another man, carrying a stretcher. Louis gave sharp orders, and Angela was faintly overawed by the authority of the man who could reduce these people into a state of obsequious obedience. 'What are you going to do?' she asked.

'The back seat of the car folds down and we can take him to Bizerta, but the hospital there might not be able to help, so it may mean a trip by plane to Sousse.' He shook his head. 'I hope they can take him, as I don't like the tension of his pulse, and a flight would be trying for all of us.'

Angela put a hand on the man's brow and found it damp and cold, but the thigh was burning hot and his pulse showed high fever. His sunken eyes showed dehydration and the water jug was empty and dry, as if it had been like that for hours. She tucked her linen hat into her bag and slung the bag by its strap over her shoulder, leaving her hands free. 'Do you want me to dress the wound now?' she asked.

'No, speed is essential.' Louis took out a sterile disposable syringe and drew up a large saturation dose of antibiotic. He handed the syringe to Angela and the orderly gave her a spirit-soaked swab. 'You do it.' He grinned. 'Nurses do this much better, as they have more practice.'

Angela swabbed the skin on the healthy thigh and injected quickly, deep into the muscle to make sure that the drug was distributed well, and massaged the area to lessen the discomfort. She was ridiculously pleased to be involved and was aware that Louis was now smiling. 'Now what?' she asked. Mustafa stopped groaning as if he knew that he was being helped, and his wife stirred herself to push a few things into a carpet-bag for him to take.

The car was cool, and Angela wiped the moist brow with clean tissue, padded the injured leg with cushions to keep it still over the bumps in the road, and forgot that this was a foreign country or that she was half in love with the man who now drove fast but skilfully back to Bizerta. The town loomed up at last and the car stopped in a wide courtyard by a modern building. As soon as the handbrake was on, Louis jumped out, barked an order for her to stay with the patient and ran into the building.

Five minutes later he came out, followed by two men with a trolley. 'They'll take him?' she asked.

'Only if we do the operation. They don't want another death on their books, but if we botch it and he dies, they can shrug and say we brought him in dead.'

'Do you work here at all?'

'I have an eye clinic here every two months, but that only gives me the privilege of getting a bed for this man. Anything more is impossible if he's not one of my eye patients.' He laughed. 'Cheer up! I may be an eye surgeon, but I haven't forgotten all I learned as a registrar in London. Imagine yourself back in that elegant hospital in Mayfair and we'll do a fantastic job.' His smile was warm and a trace of tenderness made her blush, but it was gone as quickly as it came and he turned and told her to follow him.

The theatre was modern but basic, as if used for minor casualties. 'May I see?' Angela said as the orderly lifted a tray of instruments from a steriliser. She put on a mask and gown and asked for a cholecystectomy scoop and stronger probes and a supply of tulle gras or a similar jelly-soaked sterile dressing to stop the gauze packing from adhering and so lessen the pain at the next dressing.

Louis translated and the man brought them quickly, together with a local anaesthetic spray. 'Good, Sister,' he said crisply, reverting to the formal address.

'We had a gunshot wound from a gang fight one night in Cas and the scoops were useful as the bullet was deeply embedded,' she explained.

The man groaned slightly as the spray was applied, but when the doctor had scrubbed he was silent again. The scalpel traced a line down the inflamed thigh and the man fainted. 'Good,' Louis remarked heartlessly. 'Now I can really probe. When he wakes up, it will be over.'

'Are you sure?' Angela looked anxiously at the grey sweat and the slack mouth and the whites of the patient's eyes showing under the half-closed lids.

'If not, it would be the will of Allah,' said Louis, holding aloft the bullet.

'Praise be to Allah,' Angela murmured, and cleansed the wound well with antiseptic and packed it with the sterile petroleum jelly and balsam of Peru. Louis showered the first piece of gauze with sulphonamide powder and left her to apply a firm dressing and an expert bandage.

Angela stood back and placed her soiled gloves carefully in the waste bin. The doctor did the same, agreeing that they were far too infected to be repacked, however well they were sterilised. Already the orderly was swabbing the floor with clean-smelling disinfectant, and it was a relief to scrub her hands thoroughly and plunge them into a bowl of antiseptic.

Louis dried his hands and watched her do the same. He turned to her in the confined space of the scrubbing bay and took her hands in his, bending over them as if to kiss them. I'm glad I'm here, she thought, a thrill of anticipation spreading over her body. Just to work with him is bliss, but maybe later. . .

'That went well,' he said.

'It's my job,' she replied modestly.

'Of course.' He appeared surprised. 'But I have to make sure you have no abrasions on your hands. After a case as foul as this, we have to be careful. I want you in good shape tomorrow if you're to be any good. Come on, we'll fly back to Sidi and check our other patient, and then you deserve some food.'

CHAPTER FOUR

'I INSIST that you dine here with us,' Vassila said firmly. 'Poor Angela was made to work instead of looking at the shops in Bizerta, and now you want to drag her away to a restaurant! You can eat better here, and we want to hear all about your brother, Angela. Besides, Aysha was promised an hour of talk and sweetmeats before she sleeps.'

'That sounds wonderful,' Angela agreed. She was tired and confused. At times, Louis was attentive and kind and made her heart do impossible somersaults, and then he became detached and impersonal as if he had forgotten her existence.

The flight back had been almost silent, and she hated to imagine what an evening in his company would be like if he was still in that sombre mood.

'I know you worry about Yasmin,' Vassila said gently, 'but you must forget her tonight, Louis, and also we want to hear nothing about the horrible things you did in the hospital today.'

Louis laughed. 'I am sorry. I have been a bore, and that is unforgivable. I obey!' he added with an exaggerated Arab obeisance. He smiled. 'I regret that I have no suitable clothes if you have invited guests tonight who will dress formally.'

'That is sad. I love to see handsome men beautifully dressed, but tonight our guests are French and are not being formal.' Vassila sighed and her eyes were misty. 'I wish my husband were here and could support me in matters of traditional dress. I wish to wear a *haik*, but alone, I shall feel, as you say, out of it. You have your clothes for Sousse?' she asked.

'Of course.' He glanced at Angela. 'But tomorrow I had planned to wear jeans and a cool shirt. It might be better.' –

Vassila shook her head. 'What will your patients think if they see a man in jeans when they expect to see an important doctor of Berber blood who will understand their needs and thoughts?'

'Do clothes matter?' he asked a trifle stiffly. 'They know me as Dr Joudet, who tends them as well as I am capable.'

'They know you as Dr Husain Joudet and my dear friend.' Vassila turned the palms of her hands upwards in delicate supplication. 'Wear the *gondura* for me tonight, Louis. My father used to wear it because it is the most comfortable leisure wear for a businessman, and Ali wears it when he is here. It is very beautiful on any handsome man. It would give me so much pleasure,' she added.

'How can I refuse?' he said, and forced a smile.

'I'll go to change and then bring Aysha from her room,' suggested Angela. 'That will give her more time to rest before she joins you.'

She took time over her shower and washed away the aches and tiredness of body and mind. She found a dark green silk scarf to catch back her shining hair. It matched the simple silk suit and open-toed shoes, and where the low cleavage curved over her breasts her skin was clear and pale and soft. It was too hot to wear even a slip under the silk jacket. From her case, she took a thin gold chain on which a Victorian gold sovereign hung and dropped the coin into the divide of her cleavage. The scent that she dabbed along the line of her waist under the skirt band and behind her ears smelled of musky rose and drifted after her when she went to find Aysha.

The child tried to talk in English and French in her excitement as she told Angela of her plans to ride once Jean-Louis gave permission. 'We will ride to the Oasis and bring back spices for Maman,' she cried, 'And I shall wear jeans like the girls in London, or English jodhpurs. My father has many good Arab horses,' she added with pride.

'I may not be here,' Angela pointed out. 'I have to go back to London soon.' She took her hand as they walked down the stairs from the roof garden where Aysha had been resting under an awning.

'No! You must stay here for ever,' Aysha exclaimed with passion. 'I need to practise my English. Tell her she must stay for ever, Uncle Louis!'

Angela started. The man in the diaphanous white robe was Louis Joudet, but surely he wasn't the man by whom she had sat on the plane and who she had assisted in the clinic? This man had the looks and bearing of a sheikh and his proud head was held high as if defying her to think otherwise. The dark blue eyes flashed as she approached, and she couldn't decide if they held admiration or just cool assessment in their depths.

He bowed slightly and laughed when Aysha ran to him, pulling on his hand and begging again to make Angela promise not to leave them.

'She may want to go back to the UK. We can't take it for granted that she will grow to love our country.' He half turned to make room for Angela to walk with them. 'You smell delicious,' he said, and was once again the attentive Frenchman with an added sensuality that made her blush as he glanced at her.

'I wondered if I'd used too much, but I wanted to rid my nostrils of the smells this afternoon,' she said.

'You are like a waft of orange blossom on a hot night,' he told her.

'Do pretty phrases come with the clothes?' she asked, hiding her pleasure under lowered eyelids.

'Everything flows more freely,' he admitted. 'One half of me welcomes traditional Arab clothes as easy and cool and practical, labelling me as an Arab of some importance when I work among Arabs, but the other side of me makes me take a second look in mirrors and shop fronts to make sure I am not wearing fancy dress. What do you think?' he asked.

'It looks. . .right,' she said, breathing deeply. If only he could have come to dinner in a T-shirt and crumpled jeans and been as abrasive in his manner as he had been when she couldn't run in high heels in the heat, it would be easy to talk to him. How can I sit by this man and talk about trivialities when he looks like this, making my body weak with dangerous desires and making me long for his touch? she thought.

But it was not to be like that. Vassila sat Angela between the two Frenchmen and left Louis to amuse the wives, who looked enchanted to sit on either side of him and be flattered and teased. Angela could only guess at the charm and subtle humour that made the women blush and smile. As well they might! she thought jealously.

Aysha chattered like an excited little monkey and grew flushed and warm, until Angela whispered to Vassila that the child should be in bed. 'I'll slip away with her so that the dinner party isn't disturbed,' she whispered, and Vassila nodded gratefully.

'You are kind and very tactful,' she said. 'Tell her I shall come to say goodnight later, but I hope to find her asleep.'

Aysha followed obediently as soon as the guests moved away from the table for coffee. Aysha washed and cleaned her teeth thoroughly after eating the sweetmeats that she loved so much and chose a book for Angela to read to her. Angela smiled. So *Black Beauty* was as popular here as it had been when she was a child in England!

'Read me the happy bits,' Aysha asked. 'I cry if I read about poor Ginger when I'm going to bed.'

For half an hour, Angela read the book in French and watched the child grow sleepy, then she closed the book and switched off the lamp, putting on a dim nightlight before kissing the girl's brow. I'm getting too fond of her, she thought, but it was easy to love the sweetness and impulsive manners of the dark-haired little girl.

Carefully she walked from the room, as quietly as her shoes would allow. Outside, in a cool square alcove surrounded by windows, a low table was set with coffee-cups, and as she touched the silver coffee-pot Angela drew her hand away sharply from the hot surface. A tall figure emerged from the shadows and motioned her towards a settle against a window. 'You missed coffee,' said Louis, 'so I asked for some to be sent here.'

'There was no need——' Angela began.

'No bother,' he said, and smiled. 'Vassila has things to discuss with her guests, and I volunteered to look after you.'

'I see. It was a kind thought,' said Angela, wondering if he was annoyed that his flattering audience had been taken from him, leaving him to entertain the professional nurse who was necessary but not a part of the household. He poured coffee for two and sat by her side, gazing out into the night. 'Is that music from a hotel?' she asked to break the tension between them.

'That café is half a mile away, but the sound carries on a still night.' The wailing cadence spoke of sadness and forsaken love and of loneliness to the girl who sat outwardly poised, with her fair hair shining smooth and her dark green suit making a pool of cool shadow under the ceramic light shades in the ceiling. 'You wear green?' he said in wonder.

'You don't care for green?' she asked.

'I love green,' he replied, and she lowered her

gaze. 'It is right for you as it matches your eyes, but here, it is unusual for women to wear green. It is the colour of Islam and worn mostly by men who can claim the name of Sherif.'

'What's that? Some kind of sheikh?'

'Not exactly. It is worn by men who have descended from Mohammed the Prophet through the incomparable Fatima. We wear it in our turbans or in our robes.'

'We? Does that mean you're a Sherif?' Angela queried.

He laughed. 'It means nothing. Many men claim such distinction, just as social climbers in Europe claim a coat of arms to which they have no right.'

'But you do have that right,' she persisted, and the fact did nothing to bring him close. Tonight he was an Arab of high rank, and even the way he drank his coffee seemed different to her and somehow alien.

'Fatima was a long time ago,' he said. 'I have no idea if my claim is good, but it is useful when I treat nomads who are suspicious of modern medicine and who respect me enough as Sherif to submit to surgery or treatment.'

Although he had tried to make light of it, she knew that he was proud of his Berber heritage. I'm falling in love with two men, she told herself. One will use me as a hospital sister, making any demand on my skills that he thinks he needs, and this other man, whom I met tonight for the first time, is dangerous. I can never treat him lightly. In his eyes,

she saw a dark glow while he watched the curve of
her mouth and the delicate colouring of her cheeks.

He put down his cup. 'Shall we walk in the
garden?'

'I'm rather tired,' she said.

'I am too, but we must be fit for Sousse tomorrow
and the air will make us sleep well.' It was an order,
and she rose to follow him. The rich scent of orange
blossom came from a tree dark against the night.
Louis reached up and picked a golden fruit to which
the green leaves still clung. On the same tree was
blossom in soft creamy sprays, and he picked one of
them, giving it to Angela for her to inhale the
perfume. The waxen petals reminded her of
weddings.

'This is our main crop,' he explained. 'We have
very little oil, unlike most Arab states, but we grow
fruit and grapes for wine, which we export, although
some people here drink it and are not rigorous
Muslims. Some drink wines and the local liqueur
made from figs, called Bukha. I really don't advise
it,' he added, with a smile. 'In my opinion, it's the
pits!'

'Even the wine?'

'The wine is delicious, and I must take you to one
of the places with a first-rate cellar and good French
cuisine.'

Angela looked up. It was a shock to hear the
Frenchman talking and turn to see the Arab beside
her. 'What is Sousse? Another small town?'

He laughed. 'It's surprising how little you know

about my country. I thought that Sousse was well known.'

'As I was dragged here at a moment's notice, I didn't have time to do my homework,' she said with a touch of annoyance.

'I'm sorry, I didn't mean to laugh at you.'

'But you *are* laughing at me. How much would you know about, say, Ireland?'

'It rains a lot.'

'Well done!' she said drily. 'And I can make a guess that Sousse is hot and arid. Is it like Tunis?'

'Wait and see.'

Angela regarded him with amusement. 'We shall be busy tomorrow, or so you say, and I know from experience that when a clinic begins it never ends on time. There are always latecomers who just *have* to be seen, so when shall I have time to see Sousse?'

'You are right. I must tell Vassila that we shall be gone all day,' he announced gravely.

Angela breathed deeply. 'It may not be important to you, but I have been employed by the ben Ksar family to look after Aysha.'

'You are here, and that is all that matters,' he replied calmly.

'That's no answer!'

'Believe me, it is,' he said softly. 'You radiate peace and coolness and give confidence to Vassila even when you are not with Aysha. While you are here, they are happy for me to do as I have been trying to do for a long time. That squint, although it is slight, would be embarrassing if Aysha went away

to a boarding school. Many children from diplomatic families go to school, and she might meet
children from countries where a squint is thought to
be bad luck, a sign that the child can cast evil spells.
It is a sign of the evil eye, and Vassila knows this,
but has never had the courage to make Aysha
endure what is really a minor operation, as you
know.'

'I had no idea it was so important,' said Angela.
She shrugged. 'I suppose it's better for me to be
fully occupied rather than to feel I'm wasting my
time.'

'You are not wasting your time, Angela,' he said,
and she knew that his eyes were growing darker and
more intense.

'Do you want me to wear uniform?' she asked
briskly. Tomorrow might be possible if she kept to
professional subjects.

'Whatever you think is suitable. Not uniform, but
something that covers your arms and shoulders if
you can.'

'A shirt and trousers and the leather sandals I
bought in the village?'

'Fine.' The sounds of the sea now came clearly as
they walked closer to the shore. Louis glanced at
her in the silvery light that was partly starlight and
partly from the soft lights strung among the trees.
Music and the murmuring of stirring leaves and
water mingled, and the shore ran in a golden
crescent, slightly phosphorescent and magical.

A light moved slowly across the water, a dark
square sail came behind it like a bat's wing, and the

man and woman on the beach drew closer together. A nasal song came from the boat. 'They sing of a good catch,' Louis told her. 'The light attracts the fish.'

Angela held her breath, poised on the brink of a dream. He held her hand as they walked the cool sand and watched the water surge over the rocks. In warmth and fragrance the past was forgotten, and the future beyond this place had no meaning. She was alone on a beach with the one man who filled her heart and mind with longing and dread, and she knew that he was not for her.

Louis seemed to wake from a dream, but she dared not believe that it was her dream too. She turned away, but his arm slid round her shoulders. 'Thank you for today,' he said softly.

'I must go,' she whispered.

His mouth brushed the glossy hair. 'Cool as gold and smooth as pure silk,' he murmured.

'Blondes are notoriously cold,' she ventured with difficulty, trying to sound calm.

He kissed her cheek, his lips finding the line of her chin and the dimple there. 'Gold and silk always warm to the touch,' he whispered. His mouth found hers and she trembled with the sweetness of his kiss. She knew that his hands held her body close to his and that the robes he wore were as a wisp of cloud between them as her skirt moulded to her own body in a thin veil. Heaviness threatened to envelop her. She wanted to succumb to this dangerous sweetness but something in her last hold on reality made her cry 'No!'

She felt his lips again on her throat as his teeth found the slim gold chain that led to the gentle cavern of her breasts. He pulled the chain slowly from its resting place and the gold coin glittered in the dim light. She backed slightly, her hand on her bare throat, and the chain snapped.

As it snapped, they seemed to recover their composure. Louis held the coin and examined it. 'I'm sorry,' he said, but she couldn't tell if he was sorry he had broken the chain or that he had kissed her. He laughed. 'At least it isn't a locket containing the pictures of your lovers.'

'I have none. I don't believe in such luxuries,' she said. 'That's a sovereign. It's always prudent for a girl to have some cash available in case she has to walk home.' Her attempt to put their relationship on a casual basis was working. Nothing had changed. The men in the boats were still singing, the nets glinted with a silver harvest and the stars shone down.

'I can see it's a sovereign,' he said, and she saw the white teeth flash in a sudden smile that held tenderness and not desire. 'Queen Victoria doesn't look amused! Come on, it's time that little girls were in bed. . .alone. We have work to do tomorrow!'

At the door of the house, he left her, turning away sharply. 'I need more air,' he said abruptly. 'Can you be ready by nine?'

'Of course.' As she walked away, her head was held high, but as she reached the stairs her shoulders sagged. It had been the kind of romantic interlude that would have happened to any two people coming together under the stars. A warm beach under a sultry sky had worked its magic, but now Louis was thinking not of her but of his work tomorrow, and maybe of his sister. Miserably, she wondered if he had kissed her deliberately, to make her less lonely in a strange land and to persuade her to stay with Aysha.

She felt for the familiar chain round her neck, and remembered that it was broken and that Louis had not given it back to her. Thinking he might have dropped it on the sandy path, she turned back and retraced her steps to the beach, her footsteps soft on the sand. The wall of the garden came between her and the beach path, and she looked over it to make sure that she was unseen, suddenly shy.

Louis was seated cross-legged on the sand, his dark profile carved against the night and the white robes gathered closely around him. He swayed slightly and his eyes were closed, and Angela stole away, sensing that she had no part in his sad thoughts. She imagined that she heard again the sorrowful cry of the *muezzin* that she had heard at times of prayer since she came to Tunisia, and once in her room she gazed out at the stars and the shape of the minaret from where the faithful were called to prayer.

Vassila tapped on the door. 'Did you see Louis?' she asked.

'Yes, he brought some coffee for me,' Angela replied.

'There was a telephone call for him.'

'He showed me the path to the beach, and I think he's still there,' said Angela.

Vassila glanced at her sharply. 'You were alone on the beach with a man at night?' She laughed. 'I forget that you are English and have no fears of such things. Also I think that your family cannot object if you are seen with a man without the company of another woman or a family friend.' She shrugged. 'Here, it is different. In another two years, Aysha must go to school to be safe, or have a companion to be with her at all times. We are more practical in this country and know that all women must be protected from men who have desires that must be denied until marriage.'

'Do you want me to call Louis?' asked Angela, as if she could do so quite casually.

'No, it can wait. It was his mother, who is very angry with Yasmin and I think also with Louis.' She laughed. 'I remember a time when she was so very French and liberated when her husband was alive and she mingled with the French community, but now she dresses like a Bedouin nomad hung about with gold chains as if to advertise her husband's wealth. Tonight, she was cross that Louis didn't go to Tunis to meet the woman she has chosen for him.'

A servant came to the door with a tray. 'I didn't ask for anything,' said Angela.

'I ordered tisanes and sherbet for us, and I can eat cakes when my husband is not here to tease,' said Vassila. Angela sipped a tisane of orange flowers and spices and heard in a mist what the older woman was saying. She heard about the old days in the diplomatic service when families were safe, and tales of the family from which Louis came.

'Yasmin refuses to meet the man chosen for her and has been writing to Karl again. He asked for her in marriage in a very correct manner, but Madame Joudet sees her heritage slipping away and has neither a son nor a daughter willing to carry on the old traditions,' Vassila told her.

'Tonight, Louis seemed entirely Arab,' said Angela.

'No. To me he was a Frenchman with attractive additions.' Vassila smiled. 'All men are vain, and he knows well that he is very, very attractive to women.' She looked at Angela with a very serious expression as if her reply was important. 'Do you find him attractive?'

'He's a very handsome man,' Angela admitted.

'That is not the same. A picture is handsome but lacks warmth, and he has warmth.'

'Do you think he'll marry the woman chosen for him?' Angela asked through dry lips.

'She is beautiful and has much wealth and property, but she speaks nothing but Arabic and a few words of French and has had little education.' Vassila smiled. 'Louis has had many women friends, but never one to whom he gave his heart, unless she is in London or Paris, and I have not heard about it from my spies. I wonder why he waits?'

'I suppose it depends on how much his roots mean to him. He may be torn both ways,' Angela said carefully, as if convincing herself as well as Vassila. 'He mentioned the green of Islam and his great pride in his Berber ancestors.'

'For sons of Fatima, green is a holy colour,' said Vassila, then, as if discovering something, 'You wear green!'

'It's the colour worn by blondes with green eyes and by redheads in Europe,' said Angela with a smile, as if she attached little importance to the colour.

'It would be safer to wear blue,' said Vassila quietly. 'I shall leave you to sleep now. I think that Louis will expect a lot of hard work from you tomorrow. Do not let him exhaust you, and tell him he is expected here to dine again tomorrow. He is not in Europe now, and we must take care of you,' she added cryptically. 'He is a hard man when he wants.' She yawned. 'I shall not wake early, and Aysha will stay in bed also. Breakfast will be on the terrace early.' She giggled. 'Do not tell Louis about the phone call—it could make him bad-tempered. Why ruin your day?'

Her light footsteps faded and Angela heard her talking to a man. The house became silent, and Angela listened in the darkness. She was almost certain that Louis would not try to come to her room, but she heard the swish of light garments across the hallway and a long pause close by before the sound began again.

Hating herself for not trusting him completely, she turned the key in the lock before preparing for bed. Why should he marry when he had so many friends, and even Vassila and his family could have no idea of any private sex life he had away from Tunis?

The haunting song of the fishermen came faintly as they went to sea again and invaded her dreams, and when she woke at dawn she listened for them, but they had gone.

CHAPTER FIVE

In spite of the discomfort, Angela knew that she must not give in to the urge to rub the sudden itch under her mask. One look at the clinic had been enough to convince her that full infection precautions were vital, and now, after four long hours of continuous work, cleansing discharge from eyes and ears, she was tired and suffered the psychological crawling sensation of the skin that makes doctors or nurses imagine that the infection has caught up with them too.

Dr Joudet was tireless and showed no sign of slowing the stream of men, women and children who had waited patiently for the clinic to open, having faith that their Dr Husain Joudet would help them. To him, they were people in need who had travelled long distances in uncomfortable lorries, on camels or in overcrowded louages, the communal taxis that only functioned when there was no room for even an extra child inside. The doctor swept by, his robe flapping behind him, and seemed unaware of the pale woman who had worked so hard and was even now collecting another case history with the help of an interpreter.

Angela felt completely limp. 'Is there a chance of a break?' she asked desperately.

'What? Oh, there's plenty of time for that.' But

he did stop and glance at the gold watch on his wrist. 'Good grief, is that the time? Why didn't you tell me it was so late?' He put the sheaf of papers down.

'It *was* rather difficult to catch you in flight,' she said coldly, 'but if I don't eat soon, I shall need reviving.'

'It's been a good morning,' he said with evident satisfaction. 'I can't think when I've got through so many cases. Be sure to scrub thoroughly and soak your hands in that sublimate solution, and I'll be with you. Just let me tell the orderlies what to do while I'm away. They can do the minor dressings and see people who are just here for checks after operation. If there's no discharge they can go home.'

'Scrub? What do you think I've been doing all morning?' Angela looked ruefully at her reddened hands and scrubbed them yet again. But he had gone, and as she carefully inspected her hands for abrasions, she counted up to ten and decided she wouldn't lose her temper. He's using me, and I have only myself to blame for consenting to come here, she thought. A kiss in the starlight is supposed to keep the little girl happy and willing to work herself to death! Slave labour hasn't gone out of fashion, she thought, and smiled reluctantly. There must be dozens of women who would do just what she had done, to be with him, to touch him and sense his masculinity and perhaps make him smile.

'Ah, well! If I wanted to work in a nice clean ward or a well organised outpatients', I should have stayed at home,' she murmured, but she was still sore. 'Of course he got through a good number of patients—I saw to that! And he didn't have to supervise that gangling no-good orderly in the fez who prodded and pulled instead of coaxing dirty dressings away and who isn't too fussy where he leaves filthy swabs!'

'Ready?' There he was, cool and composed as he had been all morning. Angela nodded, still too upset to speak coherently. 'I see you're a little upset,' he said. She put on her dark glasses. 'It's inevitable at first, and I do see the worst cases here before they go for surgery. Trachoma is rife in sandy countries, and we can't prevent it while the Bedouin tribes still travel nomadically and come here only when the condition is well advanced.' He smiled as if she must agree with everything he said. 'I do see that it's traumatic to see so many cases in one place.'

'I have nursed trachoma and seen far worse than you have here,' she said stiffly.

'I could see you have,' he said in a placating tone. 'You've no idea how good it is to have someone trained who can be trusted.'

'But you must have trained staff here to cover the bulk of work you do. You really couldn't have managed without me or someone well trained today,' Angela said shrewdly.

He coughed slightly. 'Well, yes, but the two male nurses are away—one is off sick and the other on leave. They're both with VSO.'

'So you planned all along to get me here to do

holiday relief, knowing that the agency would never allow it? I obviously did the work of two nurses?'

He reddened and brushed his thick dark hair away from his face, but seemed to think no apology was needed. 'You were a great help,' he said as if that was enough. 'Come on, I thought you were hungry. We can grab some food here. Most of the dishes are Tunisian, but you can have a rather tough steak if you prefer. The coffee is rather good.'

'I'll have what you have,' she said. 'And I need a glass of wine,' she added firmly.

Louis glanced down at his robe and frowned, but ordered her wine with the couscous and baked fennel root, and he drank fresh orange juice. Angela looked about her. Apart from a party of tourists, she was the only woman in the café. She was certainly the only woman sitting with an impressive Arab in traditional dress. The food was delicious, and they ate in silence until their hunger was satisfied.

'I had no idea the food could be like this in an ordinary café,' she said at last, recovering her poise and humour now that she was fed. 'I've heard so much about bad food in hot countries that I'm very pleasantly surprised.' She stretched out her arms in the sun and the pale blonde fluff on her forearms, where she had rolled her shirt sleeves high, was like a haze of illusive gold, and he took in every detail, his eyes hooded and watchful.

'You should eat where the locals eat, as in every country,' he told her, 'but you couldn't come here alone.' He grinned. 'You'd have to eat in a tourist hotel where they serve up a mess of semolina and meat and call it couscous, or have European food.'

'You can't be serious! I feel perfectly safe here. I could walk and explore the town until you're ready to go back,' she said with a brittle smile.

'But we have work to do.' His slightly indulgent smile faded.

'*You* have work to do,' she corrected him. 'It's now three o'clock. I came to help you this morning and I've worked for nearly five hours, non-stop in this heat. You have too, and I think it's enough.'

'I thought you'd be interested,' he said mildly.

'I am, but a five-hour clinic is enough and I still have duties with Aysha when I get back, the work for which I thought I was employed. As it is, I must shower and wash my hair and make sure I change all my clothes and carry no hint of infection back to her.'

'Aysha is a fairly easy stint, as I seem to recall you saying.' His sarcasm was wounding. 'Very well, I shall go back, and you can see the town. I'll meet you here in an hour, so you won't have time to go into the Medina alone.'

'The Medina?' Angela queried.

Louis sighed as if trying to make a rather dim child understand. He raised a hand and the waiter came. After a brief exchange of words and some gesticulation, the man came back with a tourist map of the town. 'We're here,' said Louis. The fair head and the dark were close together and at any other time it would have been bliss for Angela to feel his arm touching her, but mutual annoyance now made them at odds with each other.

A small boy with artless dark eyes sidled up to a British couple who had just finished their meal. 'You want a guide to the kasbah?' he asked. The man shook his head and the woman turned away. 'What have I said to make the nice English lady cross? You are angry with me, and I want to help.' He smiled sadly. 'I do not want you to be cheated. I will take you safely and keep the bad people away.' The woman looked embarrassed and the man shrugged and gave in. He nodded.

'They have a guide,' said Angela. 'Is that a good idea? The poor little boy looked so forlorn when they refused.'

'My poor darling innocent! They all do that, knowing the British sense of fair play. They make people feel guilty and think they've been rude to one of the locals and, then are made to pay them for a service they don't need.' Louis turned back to the map. 'If you go up there to the souk and then along Spice Alley, you'll see all the shops you want and be able to move about without being pestered. Just be firm and say no and move on. Never argue,' he added. 'They win every time if you do, and many people have gone back to their hotels with leather goods that they hardly recall buying, let alone wanted!'

'I can be very firm when I like,' Angela assured him.

He looked anxious. 'These people are warm-hearted and very friendly, but there are a few who are not, and they live in one quarter of the town. They resent the rich visitors and take every advantage of them. They are intelligent and can assess just how much you can afford by your manner of dress and the quality of your shoes. They mean no actual harm, but they can panic people who speak no Arabic.'

Angela looked down and wriggled her dusty toes in the leather sandals. 'Then they won't bother me in this gear,' she said, and laughed.

He regarded the long firm legs and the gentle curves accentuated by the tight-fitting jeans. Her shirt was light blue and simple, tucked tightly into the broad leather belt to which her purse containing credit cards and money was attached. She had coiled her hair into a tight French pleat that showed the lines of her neck and left a soft growth of baby hair at the base of her head. 'Be careful,' he said. 'If you come back with me now, I can show you around later.'

'There isn't time. I promised to buy spices for Vassila, and I also want to browse round the shops without a man tapping his shoe on the ground. If you're like Dermot, you hate shopping.'

'Be back here in an hour,' he ordered. 'You'll see loads of sticky sweets and you could buy some for Aysha. She adores them, even if they're bad for her. It's impossible to stop an Arab girl from eating them, and all I can do is to make her promise to clean her teeth well.'

He walked away, and even though Angela knew she was safe, the café seemed empty without him.

She wandered over the square under the colourful flags that were a semi-permanent display to convince any visiting celebrity they were in his honour and so saving the labour of removing them after each VIP visit.

Her dark glasses helped to preserve her privacy, and she ignored the pestering boys as if she was used to them and bored with their efforts to get her custom. Tightly packed stalls lined the alleyways that led to the depths of the Medina and the other souks. She examined delicate silver filigree and beaten brass, pottery and goatskin rugs. She bought a small version of the bright ceramic cockerel that she had seen with Louis, and it seemed to wink at her. 'We have so little time to stay, and here I am deliberately staying away from the man who'll send me away soon enough when he has no further use for me,' she murmured sadly.

Restlessly she turned to the stall spilling over with brightly wrapped sweets, bars of honey fudge and nutty candy. She bought two bags, one for Aysha and another of a less sticky variety that she could eat on journeys. The first she put in the straw basket that she had bought to take her other purchases and which now smelled of spices, and the other bag she held in her hand and selected a sweet to taste.

A side turning took her under even more festooned rugs and *djellabas*, caftans and leather stool covers, and she wandered on, lost in the Aladdin's cave of colour. The dim light of the shady alley broke as she found herself in the Medina, on a sloping path leading to a high wall with many small alleys. Goats grazed the yellow grass and old women eyed her without speaking, where they sat in doorways with small children peeping round the voluminous black robes.

It was another world, of light and blue sky, picturesque walls and strange people. A child came along the path, her bare feet slapping on the stones and her bright dress outgrown and ready to be passed on to the next in line in size. Her hair was dark and uncombed and her eyes unsmiling.

Impulsively, Angela smiled and held out a sweet to the child. She snatched it and demanded more. She glanced behind her as if expecting to be robbed of the sweet, and when she took the second one, she fled and hid behind a woman in a doorway.

Four bigger children ran down the path, demanding sweets and English cigarettes. Angela picked our four sweets and gave them one each. Two boys came from an alley and more girls from one of the houses. 'Cigarettes,' demanded one of the boys. 'More sweets!' Angela took a handful of sweets and threw them as far as she could. The scramble was terrifying as more and more children came from every crack in the rocks, hands reaching out to her, demanding and crowding her.

The women in the doorways ignored her growing distress and the children were pushing her and grabbing at her shopping bag. She tossed the rest of the bag of sweets away and turned towards the gap leading to the souk. A loose stone under her sandal made her stumble, and pain shot through her foot as a sharp flint found her heel. Two youths in leather jackets confronted her and demanded more sweets and cigarettes, and she thrust one aside and dashed towards the souk, falling into the arms of a man in white robes.

Panic-stricken, she pushed him away, and her basket fell to the ground.

Before the first youth could snatch it up, a voice that seemed to come from a delivering heaven spoke coldly and sharply in Arabic. The boys hung back sullenly and the children vanished into the houses until the slope was empty of all but the goats. Dr Husain Joudet gave an order in French and the nearest boy picked up the basket and handed it to Angela. He smiled, to gain favour. 'I didn't know she was your woman, *effendi*,' he said. She rested a hand on the wall while she removed the sharp stone from her sandal, and drew a deep breath.

Louis was very angry, but at least most of his anger seemed to be against the children who had mobbed her. 'You little fool!' he said as soon as she walked by his side. 'I told you to avoid this area. What did you expect?'

'I didn't expect to be attacked by a crowd of children just because I offered a sweet to one little girl,' she retorted.

'And they came from every direction?' His face was grim. 'They wouldn't have hurt you, but they might have stolen your bag and made you panic into breaking an ankle on the loose stones. Now, will you do as I tell you?'

'I'm grateful for your help,' she said coldly, 'but that doesn't mean you can tell me what to do in my off-duty! I didn't know this place was here until I came out into the open.' She saw that he was calmer. 'How did you find me?' she asked.

He gave a short laugh. 'A blonde woman with the kind of shape and softness that every man here dreams of possessing comes through the souk alone, and you ask how I knew you were here? I had only to say "blonde lady?" and they pointed this way with enthusiasm, even if they were ninety!'

'Oh,' she said in a small voice. 'And I thought I was inconspicuous today.'

He laughed. 'You have to be joking! No woman is inconspicuous here.'

Angela smiled uncertainly. He had at least noticed her looks, even though he ignored her as a woman at times. Did all dominant men flatter women to get what they wanted and then ignore them?

'The clinic is done and we can go back to Sidi. I shall have to leave for Tunis after dinner, but we have time now to stay here for another hour.' He smiled as if making a great concession for her frivolous amusement. 'First we'd better buy more sweets.'

'They look better than they taste,' she said. 'I have the ones I bought for Aysha and I don't want any more. I would rather look for a *djellaba* for Dermot. He wears them when it's very hot, and it would save sending a present through the post for his birthday.'

Louis led her away from the tourist shops into a tree-lined courtyard where a fountain cooled the air. A small shop had a window in which were a few well-chosen garments of superior cut and materials, and she chose a *djellaba* at a reasonable price, far better than any she had seen on the stalls.

Louis paused by a pile of silk and picked up a garment that seemed shapeless but was made of beautiful heavy cream and silvery grey silk. Another was pure white and yet another was palest pink and gold.

'What's in there?' Angela peeped into the back room and was told that there were caftans, jewellery and belts.

'Buy what you can now, as you'll have better bargains with me than if you come alone,' advised Louis.

The rails were full of dazzling silks and cottons, and she couldn't make up her mind which to buy. 'I'll think about it and come back another day,' she suggested. 'That is, if I'm here for that long.'

'I do the strabismus operation in four days' time,' he stated, 'so you will be needed here for at least ten days from now.' He eyed her with a touch of mockery. 'So you have plenty of time to recover from my slavedriving today,' he told her. 'You could even get bored with too little work to do.'

Angela blushed. He made her feel lazy and uncaring, but he continued, 'I have to go away before the operation, but I want you to make sure that Aysha is calm and happy.' He smiled now, and she couldn't help her own mouth from responding and her heart beating faster. He was so very attractive when he looked like that, warm and strong and understanding. 'Now that is real work,' he conceded. 'Aysha is still upset at times when she thinks of her father narrowly escaping death, and her own injury reminds her of that day. She can now swim in the pool, and when I come back we can take her riding on the beach.' He lifted one eyebrow. 'You *do* ride?'

'I can stay on a horse if it behaves,' she admitted cautiously.

'Good, then tomorrow you can lie in the sun and get as brown as Aysha.'

'I never go deeply brown,' she told him. 'I find sunbathing boring, so if you need my help, I'm quite willing to come to Sousse again.'

'I hated to suggest it. Haven't you suffered enough?' She blushed scarlet, and Louis smiled triumphantly. 'There *are* a few cases where I want you to assist,' he said as if he had it all planned. 'Three operations for trachoma. The men in question have a chronic condition, and all need to have the cartilage of the lower eyelids removed and the eyelashes everted or turned outwards so that they no longer irritate the cornea as they do in this disease.' Angela nodded solemnly, wondering what he would say if he knew how many cases she had seen in soldiers and oil-men who had worked in sandy countries. 'Sometimes in the early stages, it can be cured with antibiotics, but when granules like beads of sago form under the lids and cause ulcers, the cartilage platelets have to be removed, and at that stage it's infectious.'

'Due to the Bedsonia virus acting like a bacteria,' Angela said crisply, hiding her laughter under lowered eyelids.

'*Touché, ma petite*,' he said and laughed too.

'Surely you can't do them at the clinic?' she asked, horrified at the thought.

'No, this time you shall have everything laid on and not have to function in a plastic apron and a mask. In fact you will be an honoured guest, if that suits you better. In Tunis we have the best.'

'Did you check on the man with the bullet wound?' she asked.

'I telephoned while you were busy fighting off the children. He's recovering fast and anxious about keeping two steps ahead of the police once he's better. He's been identified as the thief, and I don't envy his position for the next few weeks.' He shrugged. 'We couldn't leave him like that, but I doubt if he feels grateful.'

'You did what was necessary,' she agreed.

'With your invaluable help,' Louis said softly, and she felt the old glow building up inside her. She tried to look unconcerned, but inwardly was disturbed. One glance of approval and the mere presence of this man made her helpless, ready to agree to any workload he put on her and ready to give and give and give whatever he demanded. His white robe did nothing to conceal his latent masculinity and made him appear almost regal as he strode easily up the steps to the house.

Aysha rushed to meet them. 'Maman told me that you say I may swim!' She clung to his hand, urging him into the cool corridor. 'You will swim with us?' she pleaded.

'I have to go to Tunis tonight,' he said, as if he suddenly recalled that he had something distasteful to do.

'Please!' begged the girl, and her sparkling eyes showed little sign of the injury she had suffered.

'I have to go,' Louis repeated. 'It's business, and then the day after tomorrow Angela will join me in Tunis to help in the operating theatre there.' He glanced at Angela and smiled. 'With her help I shall be back here quickly, and then we shall see if we can go riding, Aysha.' Angela nodded, accepting that he had no intention of telling the child that she was to have another operation so soon after the other.

'We'll have a lot of fun in the water,' said Angela, and was surprised at the wave of tenderness she felt for Aysha. 'Can we swim in the sea?' she asked.

'No!' The reply was curt and positive.

'Why not? Isn't the water pure?' She laughed. 'I haven't heard that you have sharks round this coast.'

'What kind of swimsuit have you?' he asked.

'The usual bikini.' She blushed. 'I would never go topless.'

'Have you a one-piece with you?'

'I don't possess one,' she replied. 'Why?'

'Then you stay in the pool,' he ordered. 'You might find a few sharks in the sea. The pool is safer.'

'Surely people swim in the sea?' Angela looked defensive.

'When I come back, we shall swim in the sea,' he

promised. 'But until then there are certain matters best left untested.' Aysha had run into the terrace room and he turned to Angela with a serious expression. 'The customs of this country make female modesty of great importance. Women are protected by their families from meeting men who might rob them of their virtue.' He shrugged and his smile was forced. 'You look at me as if I am very old-fashioned, but the facts remain, and when I am here, it becomes important to me too, even if I am more French than Tunisian back in London. Is it fair to show men beautiful bodies that they have no hope of possessing but appear to be there for the taking? The frustration of unmarried men and boys is great, and their passion is intensified if they see fair-skinned women almost naked on the beach.'

'You make a natural thing like swimming sound indecent,' said Angela. 'But I will stick to the pool while I'm a guest here.' She had a sudden need for him to think well of her in a way that she didn't expect from casual dates.

He bent to put his hands under the heavy rope of hair entwined round her head and gazed down into her eyes. She caught her breath. It was as if a white eagle swooped down and held her gently enfolded in giant wings. He kissed her brow as he had done once before, as if touching a holy relic. 'A woman's body is to be worshipped, reverenced and enjoyed in peace and beauty, and to the complete satisfaction of both lovers, but never to be snatched at or gloated over by vulgar men. When you fall in love, Angela, you will know. . .and maybe suffer a little.'

He released her and pushed the rush basket into her arms. 'Find Vassila and give her the spices before the whole place reeks of them.'

He made the Arab obeisance, smiling a mocking half-smile, and left her shattered by his words, his nearness and his fleeting touch.

She tried to laugh and to consider his extravagant phrases as an elaborate ploy to undermine her defences, as if she was just an old-fashioned romantic fool. 'Which is exactly what I am,' she confessed to her mirror when at last she was in her room and had finished her shower. She put the *djellaba* for her brother in a bag and sorted out the rest of her purchases. The cock-bird sat on her dressing-table, and his knowing glance seemed to follow her everywhere she went.

'I'm going to regret buying you if you stare at me all the time,' she said, and turned him to look out of the window.

Aysha danced in, wearing a soft cotton *haik*. 'Maman said that the ladies here tonight will be Berber, and so I wear this.' She held up one foot to show the gold bangles on her ankles, the jewelled toe rings and the one-strap sandals that showed off her pretty feet.

'You make my clothes seem very ordinary,' Angela told her, selecting a pale blue silk shirt-waister with a white trim on the revers and cuffs.

'Louis has no evening clothes with him, he says, but he didn't expect to be here today. He was expected in Tunis to meet his mother and the others, yesterday.' Aysha wrinkled her nose. 'Madame was very angry,' she added.

'He's leaving after dinner,' Angela told her.

'I think it's sad,' said Aysha. 'When I marry, I want to see the man first and fall in love with him, as my mother did with my father. Are you in love, Angela?'

'No,' she replied, too quickly. She hoped to hear more, but Aysha ran off again as she heard the other guests arriving. It began to add up. Louis's family wanted him to marry the girl in Tunis and he was trying to put off the meeting. He might be half French and fully Westernised in many ways, but he was expected to marry a woman chosen by his family.

She looked down over the shallow stairs and saw Louis bending over the hand of a handsome middle-aged woman. He was smiling as if he had no inner conflict and his fresh borrowed robes were worn with ease and elegance. What thoughts went on under the dark hair? Had he come to terms with his destiny, she wondered, or did he long for the women who were easy conquests in Europe? She recalled the time when he had been totally French and lifted her clear of the ground to kiss her on the mouth in the fashionable clinic in London. This was a different man, ensnared by the past and uneasy about the future, heartbreakingly handsome and more vital than any man she had met.

To her relief, Louis made no comment on her encounter with the children in the Medina and seemed to speak to her only when necessary during dinner. As before, she was referred to as a friend visiting the ben Ksars, and Ali ben Ksar's absence was explained by his need to clear his desk in Tunis ready to let him go on holiday to France and Switzerland in the near future.

What does my future hold? Angela wondered with growing regret. I shall meet Louis in Tunis, help in the theatre and then here with Aysha, and go back to thick carpets and the luxury of the expensive clinic. I shall work in London, or wherever they send me. She smiled slightly. He had quoted Omar Khayyam, and he was right. There was so little time to stay, and she would become as much a wandering nomad as the Berber women who followed their work wherever their flocks took them. But I shall be alone, she decided sadly.

She saw that Louis was watching her for the first time that evening, and his face showed concern and an emotion that made her heart miss a beat. She smiled as if she really had no sad thoughts, and he looked away. He left before coffee was served and smiled a general goodbye that slipped over her as if she was just another guest.

Mohammed came in as soon as Louis left the room and asked for Miss Menzies, who was wanted on the phone. Angela followed him to the study and he closed the door softly behind her. She gasped. Louis stood by the desk. 'No telephone,' he said, 'but I had to thank you and say goodbye.' He took her hand and looked down at her. 'I wonder how much you can guess?'

'You have to do what you think is right,' she said.

'Yes.' He gave a deep sigh. 'Whatever is decided will hurt someone. I have to sort out the pieces and put them in some order.'

Angela looked up, searching his face. Her green eyes were wet with tears, her lips soft and parted. If only it could be different! The agony of knowing that he was leaving to meet the woman he might marry drove a blade into her heart, and yet she was exultant. He does want me, she told herself. He might not love me as I want to be loved, but he desires me. He drew her into a tight fierce embrace, his mouth seeking some kind of promise that he dared not ask. His lips were hot and his eyes blazed with longing, and she clung to him, unable to resist the force of his kisses and the subtle power of his caressing hands, until she was faint with wanting.

'No!' she moaned. 'You have no right to do that!'

Louis stood back, his ardour subsiding. 'I thought——' he began. He shook his head. 'No, it isn't important. It can't ever be important to you.' He laughed, but the sound lacked humour. 'I can leave you safely. No shark in our sea would dare touch you! But in spite of your coolness, you will not forget me, Angela. Your body has many messages for me that you deny.'

He was gone before she could reply, and she was torn between wounded pride and anguish. How could he try to take her when he was on his way to a woman he might marry? And yet his surging passion had been real, his hunger a kind of pain, and she could now dream of the reality and power of his love.

The telephone at her elbow shrilled and made her come back to earth. She raised the receiver without thinking that it might not be for her. 'Hello!' The voice was somehow familiar. It was friendly and assured and masculine. 'I want to contact Jean-Louis Joudet. They told me in Tunis that he might be with the ben Ksar family.'

'He left five minutes ago. Try Tunis again,' Angela suggested. 'Can I take a message in case he rings this number?'

'Yeah—thanks. Tell him that Shane Winsconsin is in Tunisia.' He paused as if waiting for the female at the other end of the line to gasp and melt at the sound of the famous name. 'Winsconsin, the racing driver,' he repeated with less arrogance. 'I'm bored to the back teeth with sitting on my ass in plaster, so I came here to follow the test team doing the runs in heat and sand for the new engine.' Angela didn't speak. 'I run for Neo-Andaluce, the car firm,' he added.

Angela smiled. 'I know—they're your sponsors, Mr Winsconsin. How's the leg?'

'Jeez! I knew the voice but couldn't believe my own ears. It's the gorgeous blonde from the clinic!'

'I am Sister Menzies,' she agreed. 'I'm here with an eye case.'

'Ouch! Still the ice-cream lady? Give a little, baby doll—this is enemy territory and we must stick together.'

'I find the natives friendly,' she said. Her lips curved in a reluctant smile. Brash and slightly corny he might be, but he was certainly amusing.

'I'll bet they are,' he said with all the innuendo possible. 'But I'd be even more appreciative of your company. After all, we speak the same language.'

'Not always,' she warned him.

'To tell you the truth, I was bored rigid and thought I'd leave the big city and find Louis and you and maybe hit a few night spots together,' Shane told her.

'With the leg in plaster? You should be resting.'

'It's OK. Better than they thought: good position and off traction in a straightforward plaster. I have to wait for a new X-ray in six weeks, but I'm free while I wait, and I didn't want to be hounded by reporters if I went out in London.'

'I seem to recall that you had some stitches to that deep cut that are nearly due out now,' Angela began.

'Some of them are out, but I promised to see you here and get you to do what's necessary,' he said airily.

'You have a nerve!' she told him. 'I'm not running a convalescent home for ex-agency patients. Suppose I wasn't here when you arrived?'

'I made sure of it. The girl in reception was very co-operative, for a slight consideration.'

'Who needs enemies when we have people like her! I suggest that you contact Dr Joudet and he may be able to arrange something in Tunis,' she said firmly. 'I have no facilities here, and I'm sorry, but I can't help you.' She smiled as she heard his efforts to keep her on the line and then quietly hung up on him. He was so obvious, and in a way she hated putting him down, but men like him could be too persistent.

'You were a long time on the phone,' said Aysha.

'Hush! Private calls are private,' scolded Vassila.

'Not private,' Angela told her. 'More a series of requests. The caller wanted to contact Louis but missed him by a few minutes. He also wanted to speak to me as I nursed him in London. I told him to ring Tunis again.'

She saw from their faces that this wasn't enough. 'Mr Winsconsin is a racing driver who had a accident a short while ago,' she explained. He's in this country for engine trials and wanted me to check his surgical dressings while he's here. I believe he and Louis raced together when he was an amateur.'

One of the male guests sat with his mouth slightly open. 'You mean *Shane* Winsconsin? Not *the* Shane Winsconsin?' Angela nodded. 'You couldn't arrange for me to meet him, could you?'

'I don't know,' she said slowly. 'Louis might be able to do so, but I hardly know him. I've never seen him race and know nothing about the sport.'

'But he rang you and must want to be in touch,' the man continued. 'Please arrange this for me, Miss Menzies. I have been a fan of his for a long time.'

Angela glanced at Vassila, who nodded eagerly. Ah well, she thought, if he rings again, I can pass him on to these people. It can't really affect me.

CHAPTER SIX

ANGELA put down the newspaper. 'You see?' said Aysha, with growing excitement.

'I can see one photograph, but I can't read Arabic.' Angela tried to sound casual, as Aysha was at an age when she could hero-worship any famous man or pop star, and it wouldn't be wise to make Shane seem too attractive.

'But you do know him, Angela. You have nursed him when he was ill in bed,' Aysha added with a kind of reverent envy.

'I nursed him after his accident for one day,' Angela told her gently. 'That isn't knowing a person. Many people are at their best or worst when they're sick and it isn't safe to form an opinion of them. How do I know if he's a good or a bad man?' She looked at the Press photograph. 'He does look good here,' she admitted, 'but this was taken some time ago, and now he has scars and stitches on his face and arms and has one leg in plaster.'

Vassila smiled her approval. 'Angela is right. You must not judge a man from one photograph or from what you read in the papers. Men are vain enough without having girls like you following them about with stars in their eyes!

'But I think that you must know him better than that,' Vassila continued. 'I think you are being modest, Angela. Mohammed asked me to tell you that Mr Winsconsin had rung again, but you were in the pool and couldn't take the call.'

'When was this?' asked Angela.

'I was going to tell you when Aysha began to chatter about the photograph, and I haven't had a chance to speak.' Vassila laughed indulgently as if about to announce a special treat. 'I asked Mohammed to take his telephone number and when I consulted my diary, I asked him to get in touch again and to invite Mr Winsconsin to lunch tomorrow.' Aysha danced away to ask for coffee, and the two women were alone.

'I have to go to Tunis tomorrow to help Louis,' Angela said.

'That has been changed,' Vassila told her. 'Louis would like you to help him on the following day and have time to see a little of Tunis before Aysha has her operation. You can stay in Tunis with your brother, who has to be there on business, and come back with Louis and all the equipment he needs, plus another doctor to give the anaesthetic the day after.' She smiled tenderly. 'I can think of no better way for my darling child to have this done. You will all be people she knows and loves, and my husband made me promise to do as Louis orders.'

'Does Dermot know I shall be in Tunis?' asked Angela.

'It is all arranged,' said Vassila, and Angela had the recurring sensation that she was being organised without being consulted.

'I can stay in Tunis alone,' she began. 'Dermot

hates to be away from the mine, and he has no need to chaperon me.'

'Karl will be there too, and you must not be alone in a big city.'

'I need not be here when Mr Winsconsin arrives,' Angela said with a sense of relief. 'You can give him my best wishes, but I really don't know him. I doubt if I would like him more if I got to know him. He isn't the kind of man I want as a friend, and I hope Aysha doesn't become an ardent fan of his.'

Vassila laughed. 'He wants to meet you again. He accepted my invitation only when I told him that you would be here on that day but had to leave for Tunis after lunch.'

Angela groaned inwardly. There was no escape from this bold-faced man who was self-confident of his success with all women. At least he's partly immobilised in that plaster, she thought wryly. It must slow him down a little.

'I think he is kind,' said Vassila reproachfully. 'When he heard of your plans, he insisted that he must take you back to Tunis to your brother, after lunch. You will have tea with him in his hotel and freshen up there after the journey, before he has a photographic session with the Press, who want pictures of him with his scars and the plaster on his leg to show what a brave and daring man he is!'

Vassila laughed at the vanity of the extrovert racing driver, but from her tone it was clear that Shane had won her approval.

'I seem to have no choice,' said Angela lightly.

'I shall invite the guests who were here when they

heard about him. It might not be convenient, but they will come,' Vassila said firmly. 'Ahmed has rung me three times to hear if I have any news of Mr Winsconsin.' She raised her plump and pretty shoulders. 'We women arrange these things and then the men talk of cars all through lunch and ignore us.' She smiled. 'But they can't do without us.'

'I'm beginning to see that the women here have a lot more power than seems possible at first,' remarked Angela.

'A clever woman makes her man believe that he decides everything, but you will find that most family matters are decided by the women, and they allow their men the privilege of caring for them, spoiling them and loving them. With independence, educated women have the best of two worlds, the advantages of the new and the security of the old ways. Would you be safe with Mr Winsconsin?' asked Vassila.

'No woman would be safe with him unless he fell deeply in love,' said Angela. 'He has a bad reputation as a womaniser.'

'And is that bad? A woman needs to marry a man who is virile.'

'And the woman? How can she tell unless they make love before they marry?' asked Angela bluntly.

'Oh, *no!*' protested Vassila. 'The woman must remain pure.' She smiled. 'That is why we marry early, before damage can be done. My Aysha will be beautiful and very rich as soon as she reaches puberty, and must be protected.'

'Is that why she must go to a Swiss school? Is that any different from the old ways of purdah?'

'She will learn a lot and play games and meet people from other nations, instead of being fattened up on honey but starved of food for the brain as our ancestors did.'

'There is a difference,' Angela admitted. 'She can travel in the holidays too.'

'When Louis is married, I hope he can help us in that way. He is good with her and so strong. He is a true cosmopolitan, but should have married long ago.' Vassila sighed. 'Family tensions have delayed him, but he knows that he must make a firm decision soon.'

'Has that time come?' Angela asked through dry lips.

'He has a smile when he is alone or thinks he is unseen. I have noticed it on the faces of men who are deeply and secretly in love and who are about to make a commitment.'

'Can one fall in love with an arranged marriage partner? The girl in Tunis must be beautiful,' remarked Angela.

'I did,' said Vassila simply. 'I loved my husband when I was first introduced, and we have been happy. He was the man chosen for me, but I could have refused. I wanted him.'

'Louis has a sister who is being forced to marry against her will,' Angela said carefully. 'Is that right? Karl will be in Tunis, and I expect they'll meet.'

'Louis will make sure that no hint of scandal is breathed if she meets Karl, and you will be there with Yasmin if another woman is needed, but I think she should marry the man chosen for her,' said Vassila. 'He is kind and rich, and will give her many children and more freedom than most men give their wives.'

Poor Yasmin, Angela thought. Does she have any chance of happiness? As she changed for lunch, she looked across the garden to the distant beach where foreign tourists walked along the damp line of the tide. Camel drivers plied for trade and boys carrying baskets and tiny skin drums followed them with panniers on small donkeys, packed with cheap souvenirs. It was a country of strange contrasts and beautiful people, of gentleness and of the menace in the eyes of the children of the Medina. She shivered and turned away, and brushed her hair into a shining knot on the top of her head to keep cool in the heat. It was a country where a man as virile as Louis must take a suitable wife and ignore the heady current of desire that had coursed between them when they kissed. She remembered his warmth and the supple figure that had hardened to her softness in restrained passion.

'I must go back to England,' she breathed. 'I must leave before I lose my mind.'

'You look pale,' said Aysha when she joined her downstairs. 'Is the sun too strong for your fair skin?'

'I think I sat in the sun for too long,' Angela

admitted, glad to have an excuse for her pallor and the chill in her heart.

Aysha strutted about the room, wearing jeans and a T-shirt. 'I wanted to dress like you today, and after siesta we may walk on the beach. Mohammed will come with us,' she added as if that was essential. Angela had a sudden vision of harems and eunuchs to protect the virtue of the women. If I stay, I shall be infected with the magic of this country, she thought, and lose my independence. I may never feel safe wandering along Oxford Street again alone!

Lunch was an informal buffet, and Aysha took a three-cornered envelope of puff pastry and bit the corner off, tipping her head back so that the enclosed juices wouldn't escape. She laughed. 'Try it. You must learn to eat a *bric*, or you will have egg and other fillings all over your face. When I go to the camel market with my father, he lets me eat from the stalls, and I have *bric* and kebabs and drink sherbet.'

'It sounds an explosive mixture,' laughed Angela. 'I'll stay with things I recognise!'

Lunch seemed to go on for hours, with people coming in briefly and going away and fresh coffee being served at intervals. Angela stood apart watching the gardeners water the pampered flower beds. Soon she must wake up and find herself in her room in London or back in the misty Irish fields where she had been brought up. Her skin felt dry in the heat, and the midday call to prayer from the minaret was sad and nostalgic. The sea glinted silver-tipped over a blue as intense as the blue of one man's eyes, and she wondered if Louis was eating with the woman chosen for him.

Had he asked her to marry him? Could a woman from a sheltered background have any idea of his work, and could she smooth away the cares of bad cases when he found he couldn't work miracles? And would his body find satisfaction in the love of a woman to whom he had not given his heart?

The day wore on, and for the first time, Angela was glad to hear the evening *muezzin* call the faithful to prayer. The walk on the beach had been between the house and the nearest hotel, with Mohammed in attendance, making it impossible for her to walk in the water and savour the hot dry sand between her toes, and now, as she leaned over the windowsill, she thought, I can look at the stars, but I can't go out alone into the cool night. It was as restricting as the richly ornamental birdcages that were sold everywhere, to be taken back to Europe to cage songbirds, or for use as plant-holders or lamp bases.

If I stayed to be with Dermot, I'd have to take an apartment, she decided. Here, as the old song says, 'I'm only a bird in a gilded cage.' She laughed softly. What a hope! I don't even want to stay here in Tunisia alone if I can't be with Louis.

She woke to see the silhouette of the ceramic cockerel against the curtain, his high feathered tail fanned out and his red comb erect. Sun poured between the curtains, and she almost believed that it was the cockerel crowing up the dawn and not the *muezzin* that had woken her.

To her annoyance, and encouraged by Aysha, who was very excited, Angela found herself dressing for lunch with extra care. Aysha seemed to think that she must make a special effort as Shane Winsconsin was coming to lunch, and Angela knew that the other women would look elegant, all dressed in expensive Paris models as if they had never worn a *haik* and were entirely Westernised.

She chose a floating skirt of light turquoise that rustled slightly over its silk underslip. The deep scooped-out neckline of her shirt was flattering but not too revealing, although nothing could hide the proud swell of her breasts. The double row of freshwater pearls nestled against her skin and gave her a kind of courage as a familiar and much-loved memory of her grandmother who had given them to her, and she wondered if she had dressed too simply, but as soon as she saw Shane, she knew she should have dressed in an old sack!

'Hello, there!' His gaze was frank and bold and held none of the subtle veiled approval of the other men in the party. He came towards her, managing his crutches with skill.

'Good morning, Mr Winsconsin,' she said, holding out her hand in a formal greeting.

'What's with the Mister? You and me are refugees in a foreign country and we have to stick together.' He grinned amiably at the other guests. 'She saves my life and then forgets my name! How do you like that?'

Angela smiled stiffly. 'To the best of my knowledge I met you after you returned from the theatre, and I left long before you were off traction,' she said clearly.

'Time? What does time matter? It seemed a lot longer than that.' He gave a fatuous smile that made him look boyish.

'That's right,' said Angela calmly. 'It did seem a lot longer than that.' Vassila smiled and looked away, enjoying the exchange and Angela's cool expression. 'You've recovered very well,' she went on with an air of professional interest. 'I hope you managed to arrange with the hospital to take out the rest of your stitches.' She turned to talk to one of the other women, and saw that Shane was monopolised by the men who had a passionate interest in cars.

He moved easily on the light metal crutches, and his plaster only added to the impression of a powerful animal waiting to jump. His body was workmanlike, with sudden beauty in some of his careless movements, and he looked enough like a buccaneer to make the women of the party preen themselves to gain his approval.

Angela busied herself quietly with a coffee tray when the guests were out on the terrace and Shane was talking to a group of people obviously under his spell, but once, when she passed with a bowl of sugar for one of the women in the group, he reached out and caught her hand, even though he went on talking and hadn't appeared to notice her. 'Remember, I'm taking you to Tunis,' he said quietly, and dropped her hand as if the contact was unintentional, resuming the conversation as if nothing had happened.

His casual touch had done nothing for her, and yet he was attractive and the other women recognised his sexuality. Does my feeling for Louis mean that I shall never have a sensual reaction to another man? she wondered.

Most of the guests filtered away reluctantly, leaving Shane with enough invitations to fill a busy month if he could stay in Tunisia that long, and he promised to invite Ahmed and two other men to watch the engine tests in the desert. He was very polite to them, and Angela wondered if he wanted additional sponsorship from the wealthy Middle East.

The chauffeur arrived with the car bearing Shane's racing colours and the logo of Neo-Andaluce. 'We can't slip into Tunis unobserved,' Angela said, laughing, when Aysha kissed her goodbye and looked on enviously as her overnight bag was placed in the capacious boot of the car. 'I'll be back soon with Louis,' she promised. 'He'll come riding with us, and you must promise not to eat too many sweets while I'm away.'

Shane was installed in the back seat so that his leg could be supported and Angela sat with the driver, a member of the test team who would do the trials. 'What do you think of the engine?' he asked as he revved violently.

'Don't expect me to know,' Angela said firmly. 'I'd only notice that my gearbox was faulty if the car stopped.'

'She's beaut!' he said. 'We did the cold test and she came up roses.'

'In an ice box?' she asked, laughing.

'Of course not. We had three weeks beyond the Arctic Circle. Damned cold and slippery, but she's a great car.' They left Sidi far behind and went so fast that Angela wondered if she was included in the speed tests. Shane was very quiet, and she wondered if the lunch party had drained him of reserves of strength and that he was more shaken by the accident than anyone had thought. She glanced back, her professional instincts making her check, and saw that his gaze was fixed on her. She hastily resumed the conversation with the driver.

'Take us to the Oasis Hotel and then you can drop the car back at base as I'll be staying at the hotel for the night,' Shane said at last.

'You're staying at the Oasis too?' Angela looked at him with dawning suspicion. 'I thought you were staying with the team.' She saw the driver grin and was furious. The driving team would think she was one of Shane's one-night stands!

On the terrace of the Oasis, three photographers waited with cameras of various kinds and a video. Shane posed, stabbing the air with one of the metal crutches as if he held a lance. 'Great! Turn this way, Shane. Now lean on the car by the logo.'

He obliged with every evidence of enjoying it all. 'Who's the lady?' asked one of the men. 'Come on, get closer. Come *on*!' Angela walked slowly and stood about a metre away from the racing driver, protesting that she had nothing to do with racing or with Shane. 'Who cares? Just one for the book, lady.' He pushed her so that she stumbled closer and Shane gripped her firmly before she could back away, and the cameras clicked again.

'More,' said the voice she was beginning to detest. 'Give it sex. You may have a leg in plaster, Shane, but don't tell me you've lost your balls!'

Shane thrust away his walking aids and pulled her towards him in an iron grip, bending her backwards so that the cameras had a clear view of her cleavage, and then he kissed her full on the lips as the cameras whirred.

'You insane beast!' she snapped angrily as she pushed him, forgetting his disability. He slid back and clutched at the nearest thing to save him, which happened to be her thin silk shirt. The sound of ripping made every head turn, and the cameras worked overtime as they fell in a heap of arms and legs and plaster cast. The smug faces told Angela that the shots were very compromising. She brushed the dust from her skirt and dragged on the light jacket she carried to cover her exposed bra.

Shane was helped to his feet and given his crutches. He had the grace to look embarrassed. 'I'm sorry. I really am sorry, Angie,' he said. It sounded as if they were on very intimate terms. Angela stared at him. The only people who had called her Angie were her father, her brother and the man she had thought she loved in London.

'Don't speak to me,' she said through gritted teeth.

'Cool it,' he said quietly. 'Smile, damn you, or they'll make a meal of it if we fight here. Imagine the headlines! Walk with me into the hotel.' Angela didn't smile but walked with her head down, sensing that he knew more about the world of the media than she did.

The doors of the Oasis were wide open and the foyer was thronged with people, waving autograph books, menus and odd bits of paper for the autograph of the famous driver. Angela tried to move away, but Shane held her firmly by the arm. 'Angie? Where do you think you're going?' He gave a slow and insolent smile. 'They've seen you now, duckie, quite a lot of you, and you'll be in all the papers tomorrow. Why not relax and enjoy yourself? You have to stay with me now. They all expect it, and even if you slope off they'll think you're hiding in my suite. They won't even check! They don't want to know if you sleep alone tonight,' he added deliberately. 'They've written that column already.'

A cold shiver ran down her spine. 'You really think I'd sleep with you? I'd rather sleep with. . .a camel! It might have better manners.' She smiled brightly at the crowd and made her way to the reception desk. 'May I use the telephone?' she asked in a loud voice. The man brought her a pale yellow phone. 'I'm expecting my brother,' she said. 'Can you tell me if Dermot Menzies has arrived? We're sharing a suite.' The man shook his head. 'Then first get me an external line.' She saw that people were listening and Shane was angry. 'Can you get me the number of the Habib Clinic? I'm here to assist the famous Tunisian surgeon Dr Husain Joudet in his operating theatre, and I'm not sure of the arrangements.' She smiled as if she was confiding in the clerk and had no idea that she was being heard by reporters.

'I'll get the number, *madame*,' he said.

Angela laughed. 'I had a lift with Mr Winsconsin as Dr Joudet wants to take out the last of his stitches. Just as well he's recovering! He'll get into real trouble if he goes around ripping the shirts off unsuspecting nursing sisters! It might be even worse if he does that to women who are not on duty as nurses.' She had the satisfaction of seeing two reporters look as if they had stories they couldn't use, but of the cameramen there was no sign.

The suite was huge, with two bedrooms, and the door to the room next door was slightly open as if waiting for an occupant. That might be ready for Karl, she thought. She changed into a firm cotton skirt of blues and sage green and a cotton top that buttoned high on the front, then went down, bracing herself to meet Shane once more, but to her relief she saw him in a wheelchair being taken up in the lift to his suite on the other side of the hotel.

She sat under an awning and asked for tea. A waiter in the universal scarlet monkey jacket paused by her chair. 'Miss Menzies?' he asked.

'Yes.'

'Mr Winsconsin is having tea in his suite and asks you to join him.'

Angela gave the waiter a sweet smile. 'Would you thank him but say that I'm waiting for my brother and a friend? I would like tea here, please,' she added firmly.

She sipped her tea and waited, watching the

guests as they strolled through the terrace and the foyer. A tall man with dark hair was bending over a slightly built woman with a lovely face and jewel-bright clothes. She appeared very serious. The face of the man was hidden, but from his physique Angela knew that he was Louis Joudet.

Angela turned away impatiently. Would every man with dark hair and strong arms remind her of Louis? It couldn't be him! Unable to stop herself, she walked closer and saw that the woman was crying, not in sorrow but more with the release of pent-up emotion, even of joy. His arms swept round her to hold and protect her and perhaps to convince her that all was well. Then he kissed the wet eyes and cheeks, and Angela turned away, unable to bear the tenderness that the couple shared. She no longer wished to see that face. She dared not see Louis' beloved face. It was etched on her heart.

Her eyes were misty as she sat again at the low table. So that was how an arranged match began, with tears and relief and shared dignity. How very civilised to pledge their future with such caring resolve. She had been aware of warm friendship between the two people, and who was to say that it might not blossom into a deep and abiding love?

He held her as if protecting a child from the dark, she remembered. And all I have is his professional approval and his time for a while, with memories of what might have been, in a few brief and intense physical contacts.

'Angie!' Dermot hurried towards her and she

went to him gladly, feeling the solid touch of his hands and the slightly bristly kiss on her cheek.

'You're growing a beard again,' she accused.

'The sun makes it murder to shave,' he explained. He grinned. 'Where's Shane? I hear he arrived in fine style, complete with a blonde whose clothes he proceeded to rip from her back.' He stared. 'What's the matter? Are you ill? The sun is the devil until you're used to it.'

Angela shook her head. 'Not ill, just furious. I had to come here with Shane, and the photographers were ready. There was no way I could refuse a lift from the ben Ksars' house to this hotel.'

Dermot whistled softly. 'They took it for granted that any female with Shane was a groupie?' His face hardened. 'The bastard! I'll break his other leg!'

'It was partly an accident. He slipped and grabbed at my shirt.' She was alarmed at the anger in her usually mild brother's eyes. She bit her lip. There was no excuse for the kiss that Shane had forced on her mouth.

'He has a reputation for involving girls in situations, and when they can't back out they go along with him,' Dermot told her.

'I made it clear to a lot of people that I was here professionally and to meet you, and I was only travelling with him from Sidi.' Angela shrugged hopelessly. 'The cameramen had vanished when I said that, and I just know I'll never be able to show my face again in Sidi. I want to go back to England,' she finished with a sob in her voice.

'You can't. Every newsman in Europe would be

on your doorstep if you ran away now.' He gave a short laugh. 'Ignore him, and use that ice-maiden look you do so well, Angie. Some of my best friends have been frozen off by that cool look. Even Louis thinks you're untouchable.'

'Untouchable?' she echoed.

'He talks of you, but with a certain restraint as if his feelings are not the usual lust for a pretty woman.' He laughed. 'Some people still have hang-ups about mixed marriages and don't like to push their luck.'

'In his case it would be impossible,' she said, thinking of the girl she had seen in Louis' arms.

'That's what I mean. He knows you're locked in your ivory tower and wouldn't want him,' Dermot said cheerfully. 'Pity—he's a great guy.'

She smiled. Dear old Dermot had never been one to see what really went on under his eyes, or he'd know that it was Louis who held her at arm's length for most of the time because he was involved with another woman. 'People who work together rarely fall in love,' she said.

'There was a message for you,' Dermot told her. 'A car will call for you tomorrow morning and take you to the clinic at eight, so you'd better have an early night. We can eat somewhere and then stay in our rooms.' He smiled. 'I'll take you somewhere away from here in case I want to take a swing at Shane when I see him, and I'll be in the next room tonight if you're frightened of bogeymen.'

Angela smiled, recognising the phrase he had used when their parents died and he had tried to comfort her. It would be a relief not to meet Louis in the hotel, and as for Shane, she hated to think what she might do if she had to see him again soon. 'Darling Dermot,' she said. 'Show me Tunis.'

CHAPTER SEVEN

THE car was dusty and looked as if it had travelled for many miles. Angela walked from the cool foyer of the Oasis Hotel followed by a porter who carried her bag. Louis turned from the steering wheel to smile at her briefly. He too looked as if he had travelled for many miles. His face was drawn and his hair was damp as if he had tried to freshen up under a shower.

'You looked as cool as iced lemon,' he told her.

'Hello,' she replied. 'You look hot. I went to bed early as Dermot was too tired to go on to a nightclub. He said he'd travelled to Tunis during the previous night and hadn't slept for more than an hour or so.'

She wondered what Dermot would say if he knew that after the hotel was quiet, Shane had tried to come to her room. He had tapped on the door, but she had taken the precaution of locking it and putting a chair under the door-handle, and had even locked the communicating door between her room and Dermot's after she had heard Dermot talking in whispers to someone who had visited him after she was in bed.

It was puzzling. Silence followed the whispered conversation and she sensed that Dermot had gone out again. She drifted off to sleep and heard nothing more until morning. Shane had departed, frustrated, but not daring to make a noise as he thought Dermot might hear him.

'You had breakfast?' Louis asked, and gave her a heart-lurching smile that made her want to smooth away the signs of his strain and try to dull the white heat of her own despair. How could she sit by his side, and work with him, conscious of her love for him and sensing his male sexuality, loving every curve of his face and every turn of his body? Also she knew that sooner or later he would hear about Shane and the photographs, and she was frightened at the contempt he must then feel for her. 'I left Dermot to sleep,' she told him. 'I had coffee in the foyer.'

'Lucky man,' he said. 'Sorry about the early hour, but we have a lot to do before we get back to Sidi.'

'Did you have an emergency last night?' she asked, wondering if he had slept at all.

'You could call it that,' he said, and grinned. 'Dermot could have told you if you'd seen him this morning.'

'Dermot? He's not a doctor.'

'There are other ways of helping people.'

'Do you always talk in riddles?' queried Angela. 'I had a feeling that Dermot went out last night after I was in bed, but how did that affect you? And I didn't see Karl. I thought he was expected to stay the night too.'

'It's a long story and I'll tell you later,' said Louis. He accelerated and leaned on the horn to discourage a car trying to overtake on the wrong side of the road, and Angela knew it was useless asking more questions. They drove past rows of smart shops in Tunis and out into the suburbs to tree-lined avenues and a huge white building standing in a calm green garden. A hedge of cactus made a dramatic backdrop to the beds of exotic plants, and immaculate servants came to take the cases and to drive the car away for parking.

'I must have another shower,' Louis said. 'We'll have coffee while we talk about the cases and then I'll be fine.' He laughed softly. 'I promise to tell you all the news later.' He put an arm round her shoulders for a moment and almost hugged her, then released her. 'A lot of things happened yesterday that affect many people.' In spite of his weariness, he was happy, and Angela felt a dull ache inside, recalling his tenderness with the woman in the hotel. Once a decision was taken, a certain burden was lifted, and he had obviously made that decision and took it for granted that everyone would share in his pleasure. 'You'll enjoy this theatre,' he told her. 'Don't look so apprehensive! I assure you this place has everything.'

'Is there anything I can do while you shower?' she asked.

He turned away and she couldn't see his expression. 'If you can get me a newspaper, I'd be grateful,' he said. 'Not a local one. I want the two French papers that are printed here in a special Tunisian edition. You can buy them at the corner of the street.'

'Now?' she said in a husky voice.

'Yes, please. I'll meet you here in ten minutes.'

The walk to the bookstall was short, but to Angela it could have been a mile as her feet dragged unwillingly. The man tried to sell her *Paris Match*, *Figaro* and other periodicals, but when she said the papers were for Dr Joudet, he thrust the two he wanted into her hands and took the money. With a fatalistic despair she didn't even bother to open the folded newspapers, but accepted that Louis would read about her and jump to all the wrong conclusions.

'Not that it matters now,' she murmured as she waited for him to appear. 'I never had him, so how can I lose him?'

During coffee, when conversation was geared only to the cases and the anaesthetist joined them, there was no time for the exchange of personal news, and they drifted towards the theatre, where light cotton garments, caps and masks and boots lay ready for them in the changing-room. Angela took the thin plastic apron handed to her and pushed her hair under a deep green cotton cap. She slipped out of her sandals and selected a pair of supple theatre boots in her size from the row along the wall.

The air-conditioning made the temperature just right for the work in hand and the comfort of the staff, and the atmosphere of calm efficiency was reassuring. At any other time, she would have revelled in the good equipment and the clean lines of the modern operating theatre, but now she felt as if her boots were filled with lead and her eyes felt dry and hot.

She put the newspapers down on the table in the changing-room, and while she waited for Louis to finish reading the patient's notes, she felt a sudden compulsion to know what had been written about her. Reluctantly she opened one paper. If the sky had to fall, it might as well be now, she thought with a wry smile. At least she was alone with Louis as the anaesthetist had gone to check his apparatus and the orderly had gone to fetch the first patient.

The first paper had a brief mention of Shane's visit to Tunis, with photographs of the car being tested, and more of the team. It was an old library picture, taken before he was injured, and Angela sighed with relief. It must have been too early for the other pictures to catch the print deadline, and with any luck, she could be out of the country before the shock wave broke, as this was a weekly paper.

The other paper was a daily, and she opened it with misgiving. Tears flowed down her cheeks as she saw the pictures in all their terrible detail. It was worse than she thought possible, with Shane's arms holding a dishevelled blonde while his mouth was firmly clamped on hers. The semi-transparent bra, exposed when her shirt was torn, made her look half naked, and Angela sank on to a chair and buried her face in her hands. She cried as she had not done since she was a child.

Firm hands lifted her and crushed her to a man's broad chest, while a torrent of passionate words in French and Arabic flowed over her, offering her a wonderful and vital refuge she dared not accept.

'Delay the first case and bring coffee,' Louis ordered the assistant, who had returned and now hovered ready to assist them to gown up. Alone again, he murmured softly, '*Ma petite. . .mon amour!*' He kissed her tear-drenched cheeks and her eyelids and found her mouth, trembling and desperate for his kisses. His touch released the ecstasy she could not deny, and she clung to him, her misery dulled but ever present as she pictured his face once he saw the newspaper.

Maybe he had seen it, and if he had, then he was acting as Shane would do, taking advantage of her when she was helpless and tearful. The sad face of the lovely Arab woman was in the mist of Angela's tears, and she couldn't bear to think that after Louis had exchanged vows with this other woman, he was now behaving convincingly as if he was in love with her. He put her gently from him and reached across for the newspaper.

An exclamation that was half anger and half sorrow escaped him. He looked at the girl by his side, her green eyes deep with anguish, and his dark eyes clouded.

'Wash your face, the coffee is coming,' was all he said, and he pointed to the vanitory unit and towels. The orderly put the tray down and looked at them curiously. His eyes widened when Louis picked up the telephone and talked in rapid Arabic in a voice full of restrained passion. Although Angela couldn't understand a word, she didn't envy the person on the other end of the line.

More composed, she poured coffee, her professional coolness taking over and her grief spent. He had seen the newspaper, made up his mind about her, and that was the end of all warmth between them for ever. Louis slammed down the receiver as if he had won a battle, his eyes gleaming with satisfaction. 'We have work to do,' he said, and switched back to being a doctor. He looked at the notes and then tied on his mask, walking to the scrubbing bay. 'All right?' he asked softly.

'Fine,' she lied.

'Good. We have here a man who worked on a desert oil-rig and liked to sleep out under the stars instead of in the bunk-house. He didn't take the simple precaution of covering his face when asleep as the Arabs do, but let sand shift over him, and now he has acute trachoma.'

'Is he French?' she asked.

He nodded. 'We have three patients this morning. They wanted to be done here so that they can get back on the rig quickly without the hassle of going to and from the UK. Two are key men who are needed there and the third is an Arab who refused to leave Tunisia for his operation. Many do now, and so we fit them in if we can here.'

Angela tried to fix her mind on the blue-tiled walls of the scrubbing bay and the cream tiles of the theatre. It was a showplace with no expense spared, and a pleasure to use. The anaesthetist said that he was ready and smiled, his dark curling hair showing traces of African blood, but his face was pale and almost Turkish. He sat quietly by the patient and intubated him skilfully, the lubricated laryngeal tube sliding gently over the tongue and into the throat without making the unconscious man gag at the intrusive tube.

As soon as the tube was strapped firmly to the cheek away from the surgeon, Angela handed over sterile towels to the now cool and impersonal doctor who a few minutes earlier had held her in his arms. He clipped the towels to hide the nose and mouth and tube and expose only the eyes.

Angela handed him a swab impregnated with copper sulphate solution as soon as the self-retaining eyelid retractor was in place. He carefully wiped the inside of the lower lid, and she discarded the swab into a bowl away from the instruments.

The whole of the infected eye was inflamed and showed marks made by the roughened eyelids as they grated over the cornea. The tiny instruments used for the operation look almost too fragile and inadequate, but in the hands of Dr Louis Joudet, they were extensions of his skill, and Angela almost forgot that he was the man she loved, in her admiration for him as a surgeon.

The tiny ridge of cartilage in the lower lid was removed to take away the seat of infection and the source of irritation. The last of the ultra-fine sutures was inserted and a flood of antibiotics was instilled to carry on the work begun in the theatre. 'Do you think he'll recover the sight lost?' Angela asked.

'I think he's a lucky guy. He came to us soon enough to save that eye before the cornea was too

ulcerated, so even if his sight isn't a hundred per
cent he'll manage well enough.'

They scrubbed again and Louis talked of the
cases, as if he was relaxed and had not seen the
damning photographs. He's keeping me calm so
that I can finish the list without breaking down, she
thought, and it did nothing to ease her mind. After
this, he'll say exactly what he really thinks of me,
and I suppose I shall be put on the next plane back
to the UK.

The last patient had the dark, hawk-like features
of the southern Tunisian. He lay flat on the trolley,
his hands dark against the white sheet, and even at
rest, his face showed the pride and ferocity of
generations of desert existence. Angela glanced at
Louis, who was bending over him to examine the
eye, and she found an echo in his face. Anyone who
took Louis for a suave and civilised Frenchman
must receive a shock if his desert ancestry came to
the surface.

She shivered. Under that charm was a hint of
steel, a mind that could judge and condemn without
mercy. His arms were strong and warm, but they
could be arms that imprisoned as well as embraced.
A man such as he was would take any woman he
wanted and guard her jealously from other men and
from anything bordering scandal, but would reject a
woman who shamed him, if his love wasn't deep
and lasting. His wife would have to be, as Caesar's
wife, above suspicion.

The man on the table had only the first signs of

infection and was treated for corneal ulcers and inflammation of the iris.

'He will respond to drugs and local treatment,' Louis said. 'His pre-auricular glands are swollen, indicating an acute infection and not a chronic state, so I think we can clear up the keratocon conjuctivitis fairly easily.'

Louis seemed happy, even elated, and Angela's misery grew. He didn't care. He had used her again as a theatre assistant and now had no need to appear sympathetic. What did he care that her face was over the front page of a newspaper? She would return to England and he could forget her. She watched him peel off his gloves and toss them into a bin, then she put the soiled surgical towels on the trolley with the instruments and smiled at the girl who came to take them for clearing. There was no escape. She must join the rest of the team for mint tea or coffee, and make small talk.

Louis pulled off his theatre gown and stood by the scrubbing tap to wash the glove powder from his hands. The water splashed over his bare chest and bedewed the brown, smooth and hairless skin. He laughed and towelled himself vigorously, his dark blue eyes glinting with humour and something more that threatened to bubble up and make him explode with joy or triumph.

Three successful operations that were well within the scope of a surgeon of his reputation and experience were hardly enough to make him this happy! Angela removed her gown and washed her hands. She kept her eyes hidden. 'Can you make do with this?' he asked. 'It's not humid in here, and you can shower once we get back to Sidi.'

'Fine. I shall enjoy it more there,' she said quietly. 'Have you all you need for Aysha's op? Do you keep your own strabismus hooks or do you borrow them from here?'

'I have a complete set in the car and I have to pick up some sterile drums and lotions on the way back.'

'You don't really need me at Sidi,' she said impulsively. 'I could leave today, if that would be convenient. Vassila has so many people to help her, and Aysha won't need real nursing. I could go home and save a lot of embarrassment.'

'That is so,' he said gravely. 'It's true that this operation is a small one and could be done by any fairly competent eye surgeon or registrar. I suppose there is no need for me to be here either, but these people happen to be people I love, so I cancelled several appointments to come here and be here when I was needed. Aysha is special, and I thought you had begun to become fond of her too.'

Angela blushed. He made her seem uncaring. 'Of course I'm fond of Aysha, and I think she likes me. I wanted to help her, but now everything has changed,' she whispered.

'You are still needed,' he said severely.

'Why? In London you would do this operation alone with just an anaesthetist and someone to clear up afterwards. There is no swab count nor a need for extra instruments, and it's straightforward.'

'Let's say that I just like being spoiled,' he said,

and grinned. 'I could get used to your help, Sister Menzies.' He became serious. 'You are forgetting Aysha. She depends on you, and our first duty is to see that she is relaxed and able to cope on the way to the theatre and afterwards when once again she may have her eyes bandaged for a short time. You must be with her until she's anesthetised, dressed in something pretty and with no mask or cap to alarm her. I know just how much it will mean to many people, Angela.'

Angela clasped her hands to stop them trembling. 'That's if she wants me now,' she said softly, but Louis had gone to answer the telephone, and didn't hear her.

To her relief, her eyes were not very swollen, and she cleaned away all traces of make-up and applied a little moisturiser to her skin and a touch of pale lipstick to her mouth, but winced when she touched the bruise where Shane's teeth had caught her lip. She combed her hair back and tied it in a pale blue chiffon scarf, and waited for Louis. More mint tea was served, but he refused it. 'We must eat soon,' he said. 'I had nothing this morning and neither did you.' He frowned as he looked at the clock on the wall. 'We haven't a lot of time. I have two calls to make and a telephone call that is important.'

'Can I help?' she asked.

'Not really.' He looked at her and spoke with real regret. 'I had hoped that today would be so very different. I wanted to show the town to you as it should be seen by visitors. I doubt if Dermot was very good at that—he doesn't strike me as the perfect guide.'

Angela smiled. 'No, he hates towns, and his sightseeing is usually restricted to places both far distant and very uncomfortable and bearing traces of oil deposits or precious ore.' She wondered if Louis wanted to avoid being seen with her in public. 'We could snatch a kebab from a stall here and not go into the main part of Tunis,' she suggested, and sensed his relief. 'Aysha told me she does this when she's with her father.'

'What a good idea! Afterwards, you can look at the shops and meet me here later by the big car park. There's a stall in that side street where we can eat.'

To the casual observer, they were just a very attractive couple, enjoying an outdoor snack together. Angela was in a dream; Louis walked by her side, smiling and talking about Tunis as if he had no memory of the newspaper pictures, and as if he might even enjoy being with her.

'Try this,' he said, and handed her a triangle of flaky pastry, and she remembered what Aysha had said about eating a *bric*. It smelled delicious, and Angela put back her head and bit off one corner as Aysha had done, but even so, a trickle of egg escaped and ran down her chin.

'You're doing well,' Louis said with approval. 'You've eaten *bric* before?'

'Aysha showed me how,' she said, and searched for a tissue in her pocket.

'Let me,' he said. He turned her to face him and

wiped the smear of egg gently from her chin and from the corner of her mouth. His touch was a torment and a delight, and she wanted to tell him to go away, to go far away where the agony could no longer affect her. He bent and kissed her lips, so softly that it was like the *frisson* of a butterfly wing. She started and looked up, her green eyes filled with tears. Among the busy, noisy streets, they were alone. The stallholder was serving another customer and a huge man in an oversized *djellaba* blocked the view of passers-by. The dark blue eyes were unsmiling. Louis saw the bruised lip and his eyes were hard. 'Did he hurt you?' he asked.

'A little,' she replied. It was the first reference he had made to Shane, and her answer sounded weak, almost an excuse for the man who had forced his kisses on her.

Louis shrugged as if shrugging away any emotion he might feel. 'I hope it doesn't interfere with your eating. The kebabs are ready.' They sat on low chairs and drank fresh orange juice and ate hot kebabs and another *bric*. Louis looked at his watch. 'I'll take your things to the car and leave you free for shopping,' he said. 'Have you enough money?' he asked. It was the casual question that any man might make to a wife or sister or to his mistress, and sounded natural. Angela wondered if he had made that remark to many women.

'Plenty, thank you,' she replied. She gathered up her bag and walked away. 'See you at four?'

'Or as near as I can make it. If I'm late, there's a small tourist café where you can wait. In fact, let's meet there. It's tucked away in the shade and they serve good fruit juices there.'

But I'd better be there, wearing dark glasses so that he needn't be seen with me by any of his friends, Angela thought wryly, then smiled. Cheer up, she told herself. Tragedy queen never did suit you. Where's the funny side of this? There must be one! Maybe I shall laugh at this in about a hundred years' time.

She went into a street lined with shops of every description, wishing she could buy rugs and tapestries to hang on the walls of her flat, but they were all far too expensive for a girl unwilling to haggle over the prices, and she hated the thought of being cheated. She wished Louis were with her to get a bargain, and knew it was unlikely to happen ever again. Once the op was done and Aysha was well again, London would be the next stop, and with it an unpredictable professional future.

Dermot had not said goodbye, she recalled, and she wanted to see him again to ask what Louis had meant when he said that Dermot could have told her about the night's emergency, but when she approached the hotel she saw a man sitting on the terrace who wasn't her brother and who could have been Shane, so she fled back to the shops and safety.

Louis had made sure that she took all her belongings from the hotel when she left that morning and her bill had been paid, so there was no reason for her to return. I'll ring him from Sidi, she decided, and concentrated on buying a kaftan of dull rust and green cotton and a hand-painted scarf that would do as a gift for a friend in the hospital at home.

The scent of spices filled the air, and she bought the ones that Vassila used for cooking and then some aromatic ones to perfume her own bedroom. One musky scent held all the breezes of the country, overlaid with orange blossom and bitter herbs. She watched it being packaged and wondered if she could ever have the courage to open the packet and remember a time when her heart had broken.

At four, she sipped sherbet for the first time and decided that if she stayed in Tunisia for a very long time, she would never be tempted to drink it again. 'When in Rome?' a voice said, and Louis dropped into the chair beside her.

'Not my favourite discovery,' she admitted. 'In future, I stick to orange juice.'

'Revolting,' he said cheerfully. 'I never touch it.' His manner was crisp, and in a pale linen jacket and Gucci shoes, he was entirely European.

'I don't want to finish this if you need to get started,' Angela said politely. She followed him to the car. 'I wonder if Dermot is still here,' she said. 'I didn't leave a note for him this morning, and I know he has to get back with Karl.'

'He isn't there,' Louis told her.

'How do you know? Have you seen him today?'

'He's gone back. He sent his love and will telephone you in Sidi,' Louis said, and smiled. 'I rang him before he left.'

'Oh, I wish I'd known!' said Angela crossly. 'I wanted to speak to him.'

'He's a bit busy just now,' Louis replied with an enigmatic smile.

What was going on? she wondered. First the whispering next door to her room during the night and the fact that Dermot had gone out after pleading exhaustion, then this air of mystery. Dermot was *her* brother, not just the friend of this infuriating man. She glanced at Louis and resented his self-satisfied air of, 'I know something you don't know.' He was also driving away from Tunis as if the whole of the Camel Corps was after him, and the car was getting dustier and dustier.

The road threaded through sand dunes under a late afternoon sun that made the distance gold and vermilion on the shifting horizon. A few trees in the distance became a small oasis with camels chewing under the date palms and tribesmen squatting by a smoky fire of dry cactus and camel dung. Sidi couldn't be far away, and Angela was surprised when Louis stopped the car and opened the doors. 'Is something wrong?' she asked.

'I thought you might like to see the real desert before we go back,' he said. He locked the car and walked to the edge of the trees, looking towards the setting sun and the unbelievable mixture of colours in the sky. The sand was soft and warm, and Angela's sandalled feet sank into it. There was no path as the last winds had made eddies and banks that covered the camel trails.

Louis gave a sigh of relief.

'I thought you were in a hurry,' she commented.

'A hurry to leave Tunis. I hate cities of that kind.'

'So do I, but perhaps for different reasons this time,' she ventured.

He held out his hand and drew her down beside him on the sand. She faced him unsmiling. In Tunis, he didn't want to be seen with her in public, but here he smiled as if he expected her to come to him if that was what he desired. Please let me be strong enough to resist him, she prayed. She moved away from him as the distant call of a *muezzin* added its mournful longing to her prayers. 'What does it say?' she asked.

'It calls the people to prayer, saying that there is one God and that God is Allah. It is a deep and simple belief.'

'And do you believe it?'

'I believe in God, but neither my sister nor I are religious. My mother hates to think that Islam has lost us, but we are not wholly of her race and so my father gave us the choice.'

'No more than one wife?' Angela asked lightly.

'Only one, and that for ever,' he replied.

'That sounded like the call from the tower.'

'It has the same truth: a kind of fidelity.'

She looked away, the colours of the sky reflected in her hair. She picked up a handful of dry sand and let it trickle through her fingers, and Louis watched the pale skin against the gold of the sand as she picked up more and more, letting it slip in an obsessional stream, loving the warmth and softness and the sensation of eternity. Marble cities such as Carthage would crumble in time, as all the power of Rome had done, but this softness would come back and hide it all with the irresistible force of gentle possession.

'You are shivering,' he said.

'I'm not cold. I was just thinking of all this space. It's terrifying. It's so beautiful and vast and completely impersonal.'

A vivid band of violet faded to light rose and pale mauve, and a camel roared among the trees, disgusted at being disturbed and made to join the line ready to leave the oasis. Movement came from the camp and the smell of the spent fire was acrid on the air. Louis stood up and pulled Angela to her feet. . .'The stars are setting and the caravan starts for the dawn of nothing. . .oh, make haste,' he quoted. He held her close to his body, savouring the gentle submission of her hips, then kissed her gently, before releasing her abruptly. His voice was husky. 'Life is so short, but we must go now. Vassila is expecting us. She's worried about Aysha, and we must make everything easy for them.'

'Yes. We shouldn't have stopped here. It wasn't fair!' She spoke bitterly.

'I had to introduce you to the desert,' Louis explained quietly. His face was tense and his mouth under control. 'But to stay longer when the caravan had gone would have been very foolish.' He shut the car door and went round to his own side of the car, and she thought he murmured that she was too beautiful, but it must have been her own hopeful imagination.

They drove back to Sidi almost as fast as Shane's driver had done on the way to Tunis. She saw Louis reflected in the mirror and his eyes were tired and angry. Was he angry with her, or was he angry because he had reacted to her as any man might to an attractive woman? The difference was that he had promised to marry another woman and had no right to feel any desire for the girl who had come to nurse Aysha.

At least Shane was honest and took what he could, openly. He made no secret of the fact that he chased women, but this man was far more dangerous. His charm dared her to love him when there was no hope of that love being returned, so he could use her in his work and keep her devotion, even if he was married. If the caravan had not packed up and come closer, would he have made love to her on the warm sand, under the vibrant sky?

The lights of Sidi were bright and welcoming. Angela turned once to gaze into the deep hollow of the now black desert. Were the colours only a dream? This was real, the lights and voices, the lovely curtains and furnishings, and Vassila, warm and so very glad to see them again. Reality was also Aysha, who nearly knocked Angela over with her welcoming hug, and Louis, looking down at the child with such tenderness that Angela felt a twinge of envy.

The night was lit by stars that dotted the dark like sequins on a veil and a young moon hung low above the sea. It would be the same in ten thousand years, but she would be gone and all this would be forgotten.

'You look sad,' said Vassila. 'Has that terrible

man been working you too hard?' She smiled with teasing affection.

'She did work hard,' Louis said. 'I know we can rely on her.' Vassila squeezed his hand. To her this operation was a big event and a traumatic experience.

He glanced back to see if Aysha was there. 'I know you worry and your husband can't be here, but Angela will stay with Aysha and put in eyedrops as she has done so many times, before we inject Aysha with anaesthetic, and she will see nothing of the room or the instruments; only Angela in her normal clothes. It was a good idea to invite guests for dinner, as another doctor among them will not be noticed.'

'He came earlier and swam and got to know Aysha,' Vassila told him. 'I feel safe with you all.' She looked at Louis severely. 'What of the other matter? I received a very strange and upsetting phone call!'

Angela blushed and her heart pounded with panic. They knew! They all knew about her and Shane! Vassila was too polite to refer to the matter to her and blamed Louis for not taking care of the nurse engaged to look after her daughter, and yet her manner had not changed towards her.

'I think I'll go and change. Does Aysha need any help?' she asked.

'She has her servant,' said Vassila. 'You dress very well, Angela, but I wonder if you have something more formal for this evening? We have two important diplomats coming, and as my husband can't be here, the burden of impressing them falls to me.' She shrugged as if it was a bore, but Angela had the impression that tonight was important.

'I could have dinner in my room,' said Angela. 'I have a long skirt, but the shirt that goes with it was torn and I had to throw it away.' She took a deep breath. If any mention was to be made of her scene with Shane then surely now was the time?

Vassila showed no sign of reacting to the remark.

'Louis, she must dine with us. See to it, my dear,' she ordered. Mohammed bent to give her a message and Louis went to hear what was said as Vassila looked anxious. 'Now?' she queried. 'It is ridiculous! We are about to change for dinner.' Mohammed persisted and at last she nodded. 'Very well, you may show them into the study. Louis? You will go too?'

'Of course. I will see to everything,' he said. He turned to Angela. 'Please wait. This concerns you. There is something you must do before you change. There are three gentlemen of the Press waiting to see you.'

CHAPTER EIGHT

'I'M Sister Angela Menzies, part English, part Irish. I work in a swish private nursing agency in London and this is all a dream,' Angela told herself as she dressed in the matter-of-fact jeans and crisp cotton shirt that were meant to convince a child that today was not special and that nothing could happen to upset her ordered life. 'I shall be back in London in a few days and they'll forget me.'

She put down the exquisite coffee-cup and followed Mohammed, who had appeared to take her to the room prepared for the operation, and they went along the airy corridor to a high-ceilinged room stripped of furniture except for a firm chaise-longue and a couple of tables. Behind a screen were the trolleys for the surgeon and anaesthetist, and the portable operating table. In the corner a small steriliser bubbled as smoothly as a hubble-bubble pipe.

Angela took the tray of instruments and put them to boil, then with a mask over her face she laid the trolley with sterile towels and added small dishes and a pile of sterile swabs from a drum. Only the instruments were now needed to add to the trolley, and when they were ready she laid them out in the order that they would be needed for the operation, with lotions and soft eye-pads and dressings readily available.

The other trolley she covered with another sterile towel and laid out gowns and gloves in various sizes. She covered the trolleys with more sterile towels and left them behind the screen, turning her attention to the anaesthetist's table. She checked that there were swabs and a selection of laryngeal tubes with a pot of water-soluble lubricant, and that the cylinders of gases were full and working properly. Phials of different drugs that might be necessary to induce the right state of unconsciousness were ready, and the portable machine was small and looked like just any piece of electronic office equipment. It had none of the drama of the usual hospital apparatus.

In the outer room, the couch where Aysha had so often lain while drops were instilled into her eyes and examinations had been made was ready, and just over an hour ago Angela had strapped a pad containing a local anaesthetic on to the girl's hand to deaden all feeling when the first injection to send her asleep would be given in her hand, so she would not even know an injection had been given. 'Just a skin test to see if you need extra vitamins,' lied Angela in case Aysha was conscious enough to ask why the strapping had been applied, but the child had not even noticed what she was doing.

'And after I have my drops, may we go riding?' she asked sleepily.

'Soon, when Louis gives permission,' Angela promised.

Everything and everyone bows to what Louis decrees, Angela thought as she checked the room again and saw that there were fresh towels by the washbasins and in the shower-room. Everything seemed so normal today. A man watered the flower-beds and servants laughed by the back door as a boy selling watermelons told them the latest gossip, and yet last night had been completely unreal, with a sensation of being controlled beyond her own will.

She had wondered if her feet could take her into the study when Louis ordered her to go with him to meet the reporters, but he had gripped her arm firmly as if he suspected that she might want to run away, even if flight in the darkness was impossible, with no idea of where she could go before leaving for the UK.

'You must come,' he told her.

'I have nothing to say to them,' she pleaded. 'Louis, I can't face them!'

'You need not speak if you want to remain silent, but they must speak to you,' he said firmly.

'Whose side are you on?' she murmured. 'Please let me go and tell them I've already left.'

'*Courage, ma petite*,' he whispered, and threw open the study door. The three men jumped to their feet. Louis regarded them with hard eyes, although his lips were smiling. 'Sister Menzies, these gentlemen have something to say to you regarding the gross distortion of truth they printed in their newspaper this morning.'

Angela stood quite still, unable to do more than

nod coldly. Her mouth refused to move and her eyes were wide and very green. Light from the curved window touched her hair, brushing it with innocence and making her fair skin look childlike. One of the men coughed and another went scarlet with embarrassment. It would have been easy if the woman had dissolved into tears or shouted at them, making a retort possible, but this calm dignity was unexpected and her whole bearing very disturbing.

As Dr Joudet will have explained to you——' the man began.

'I have said nothing to Miss Menzies,' Louis told him.

'Oh?' The men exchanged glances. If they had not discussed it, then perhaps the hoped-for hysteria would now come. 'We have come to apologise for the *perhaps* mistaken action of our photographers,' he explained with an ingratiating smile.

'You have come to apologise for a gross misrepresentation and to give full compensation for the libellous article that accompanied the pictures,' Louis said in a voice that seared the air. 'You have the document there?'

Reluctantly the man produced a large envelope and handed it to the doctor. Angela said nothing, because she was bemused and there was nothing she could say. There was a terrible silence while Louis took his time reading the document.

He looked up. 'On the telephone, we mentioned a sum and the text of the apology. It is to be a formal public apology printed in a conspicuous place in large print, and not hidden in a corner where the sports page ends,' he added drily.

'It's in the other paper.' The man gestured to the envelope again. 'But is it really in the best interests of the lady for us to make such a public apology? It will only make readers wonder what was said when the article appeared.' His smile was hopeful and very knowing.

'You will print exactly what was agreed,' the inexorable voice continued. 'When this lady marries, she does not want other papers picking up your dirt and smearing her name.' He read the other page, nodding approval. 'This must be printed in the next issue, or my lawyers will contact you.'

The spokesman shrugged and seemed to lose interest, knowing that they had lost. It was bad luck that this girl had the backing of such a powerful local man and the ben Ksar family who were connected with the ruling body of the country. 'Do you accept our apology, *madame*?' he asked.

Angela nodded dumbly. Louis thrust the envelope into her hands and took the men from the room. 'Sit there and study the papers,' he commanded. She sank into a chair and hid her face in her hands, and when Louis returned some minutes later, all she could say was, 'Why?' The envelope lay unopened on the table.

He took her cold hands in his and she felt the vibrant force of his magnetism flow through her numbed fingers as if he willed her back to life. 'It's over,' he said softly. 'They will never do that to you again.'

'You shouldn't have made a fuss,' she said weakly. 'I could have slipped away and it would have been forgotten in a week.'

'It was a matter of honour, and you are a visitor to our country, so that makes it a matter of honour for us too.' She smiled slightly. So it was a matter of honour for his country, and not a tender concern for a woman for whom he felt love and care. 'And a little extra money can't be bad,' he added, smiling. He reached over and extracted the cheque.

Angela eyed it with distaste. What use was money if she couldn't have his love? He thrust it under her nose so that she had to read it, and she gasped at the huge sum it showed. 'I can't accept that!'

'You can and will,' he stated. 'It shows that they are at fault, and money talks. Use it for something,' he said, waving his hand as if she might spend it all on trinkets. 'Use it to buy a trousseau.' He grinned as if the money was nothing and could be used and forgotten.

'I don't need the money and I don't need a trousseau! I'm not getting married!'

He laughed. 'I was right to keep you in the dark. With those green eyes flashing they would have been able to fight you and make you say something damaging. It was a relief to see you struck dumb!'

'Oh, *you*!' she snapped incoherently. 'What do I do now?'

'You get dressed for dinner.'

'I can't face Vassila now,' she begged. 'Please, Louis, just let me slip away.'

'When a woman has watched her husband being

shot at and nearly gunned down, and her daughter injured in the attack, a little matter of libel doesn't signify,' Louis told her. 'Vassila is far more worried about Aysha than about your little argument with the Press. Besides, she knew I would sort it out honourably,' he added, with an infuriating air of confidence.

Angela almost laughed. 'That's all very well, but one simple fact remains. I have nothing suitable to wear this evening, and that *would* affect Vassila.' She recalled her calm dignity after the attempted assassination and felt suddenly protective. Her own troubles seemed trivial and she knew that there were still duties to perform for the family she had grown to love.

'Go to your room and you will find that Aysha has something very suitable for this evening. You will wear it and please. . .Vassila.'

Why couldn't he say that it would please him, even if he didn't really mean it? He had dismissed his own part in her action against the Press, and now eyed her as if she was a bit of a nuisance and had to be firmly instructed and made to obey what he decreed. He even looked at his watch as if she had taken up far too much of his valuable time. 'I shall wear what I like,' she retorted. 'I do have some will of my own left.'

'You will, I think, please Vassila if you wear what we have chosen, and Aysha will be delighted to help you.'

Walking like an automaton, Angela went to her room, ready to sink on to her bed and refuse to move until morning, but Aysha danced out to meet her, with glowing cheeks, the slight squint much more pronounced now that she was excited.

'Come and see!' Aysha called, and Angela made a great effort to appear normal. There was still work to be done, and this was a part of it. She warmed to the girl's affectionate enthusiasm and allowed herself to be pulled across to the bed, where a shapeless heap of silk lay on the coverlet. She picked up some of the silk and let it drop again. It reminded her of something she had seen in the boutique in Sousse. The cool heavy silk flowed through her fingers in a stream of gold and palest pink, and she knew it was the same loose and flattering garment that she had seen there.

'It's a *haik* like mine,' Aysha told her in triumph. She twirled and her own sinuous garment flowed with her body, hugging it with grace and then flowing away again, showing a hint of what her figure would become during the next year or so.

'I can't wear that!' protested Angela. 'I'd never be able to keep it on!'

'I show you. First you take off all your clothes and shower, and I will wait here and read your magazines.' Aysha pulled some magazines towards her and looked at the fashion ads. 'When I come to England with you, I shall buy clothes like these.'

'So you're coming to visit me, are you?' Angela smiled. It was wonderful to be so young that anything was possible. She showered and came back wearing only her bathrobe. 'What do I wear under it?' she asked, suddenly aware that Aysha wore very little apart from the *haik*.

'Just a bikini bra and pants so that the *haik* hangs well and clings where it should.'

'I think I shall wear a slip as well,' Angela decided.

'You are so funny.' Aysha rolled on the bed. 'Nobody wears a slip!'

'All right,' said Angela, resigning herself to the girl's efforts, and they dissolved into laughter when Angela said she could manage and failed abysmally to fix the folds of the *haik*. 'I can't wear it,' she protested, but knew that Aysha was determined to dress her.

'Maman insists,' Aysha told her. 'And it is beautiful. Louis had good taste.'

'I can't accept this from him,' Angela protested.

Aysha shrugged. 'Maman said you had nothing suitable and he would arrange. It is nothing. He is good at arranging,' she added carefully, as if she had discovered a new word.

'So I noticed,' Angela said drily. Perhaps Louis had bought it for Vassila and it was lent to her for the night, but Vassila wore much stronger colours, and pale pink and gold weren't her style. She stood before the mirror, then moved to look at herself sideways. The *haik* moved with her, flattering and caressing her body, and it was only when she stood still that it hung in folds and hid the figure beneath it. 'I shall stand still all the evening,' she said, amused by the delighted expression on Aysha's face.

She brushed her hair and was about to coil it up

when Aysha stopped her. 'Leave it loose and all the men will desire you,' she said with a chuckle.

'Thank you very much, that's all I need!' Angela murmured. If there were men like Shane at the dinner, then the *haik* would be provocative enough. She compromised by pulling most of the hair back under gilded combs and letting curling strands fall over her cheeks.

With a fast-beating heart, Angela walked slowly into the salon where Vassila waited for her guests, dressed in vivid robes and magnificent jewels. Heavy golden chains hung from her neck and her bare ankles were covered with bangles of precious metals and rubies. She smiled with pleasure when she saw Angela, who murmured, 'Thank you for loaning me this lovely *haik*.'

'It is yours,' Vassila said simply. 'If you were a woman of my race you would wear all this gold, but for you the simple dress is enough. However, you should have earrings. This goes with the dress.'

Angela backed away as Vassila pressed a box into her hands. 'I can't wear heavy jewellery, it doesn't suit me,' she began, but Vassila ignored her.

'Aysha, take her and put them on.' In the ante-room, Angela opened the box and gasped. Aysha fixed the small exquisite ear-studs of emeralds set in gold, and the slender necklace that matched them exactly lay softly on her throat. It had no resemblance to the ornate chandeliers of jewels that the other women wore.

'These are precious. These are real emeralds. I might lose them!' Angela was alarmed.

'They are yours,' Aysha said carelessly, in the manner of the hostess welcoming a guest to the house with the time-honoured phrase, 'my house is yours.' Angela couldn't refuse without giving offence, so she decided to enjoy the evening as if she acted a part and would wake up after a long dream; and it would be only a dream that could never be repeated. Tomorrow, Cinderella would wake up and find the emeralds gone, the silken robe vanished and her air ticket ready to send her back home.

The evening passed in a glow of good food and fine wines and fruit juices. There were many lovely women dressed formally in the robes of their races, and handsome men in dark suits, adding a Western touch to the international gathering as many of them were business acquaintances and dressed accordingly, and not in the robes they wore less and less on formal occasions.

Louis wore a well-cut suit of a lightweight dark material and a shirt of pale gold silk that echoed the gold in Angela's *haik*. It must be a coincidence, she told herself.

Louis talked to the other guests and yet whenever she looked towards him he was watching her, his eyes slumbrous with controlled admiration. Her heartache was mixed with pride. He wanted her, even now when he was engaged to another woman.

She looked away. Frenchmen had the reputation of taking a mistress after they married if the marriage was one of convenience, and Louis was half French, but she hated the idea of being a woman in the shadows waiting for her lover to come when he could spare the time. Many Eastern countries allowed men to take more than one wife, but Louis was not orthodox and had said that for him, one wife would be for ever.

I'm fooling myself, she thought. He might have only one wife, but how many mistresses might he take after marriage to the woman I saw being comforted in the hotel? That tenderness was for real and in time would grow into real love, and with children his marriage would be all-important to him. What he feels for me is the same lust that Shane Winsconsin feels for any attractive woman he can make. It was easy to tell herself these things, but whenever she glanced in Louis' direction she could feel the vibrations of whatever it was that made him look at her, echoing her own longing, and wondered why the other guests noticed nothing between them.

Laughter and talk flowed through the elegant salon as if nothing but the night breeze from the sea disturbed them. Aysha yawned and her eyes were over-bright, but when Angela suggested bed, she shook her head. Louis had left the room and Angela needed someone to persuade Aysha to go and rest, but she didn't want to make it seem urgent. 'I spoke to my father today on the telphone and he is sending me a present as he has to stay in Tunis,' Aysha told her. 'Maman and I shall visit him soon, but he prefers that we stay here where it is safe.' She looked troubled. 'Do you think he is safe, Angela?'

'I'm sure. He is in his own country with people who admire him, and they caught the men who tried to kill him,' Angela said firmly. 'Your mother told you this, and it's true.' It was the first time that Aysha had appeared scared, as she recalled the day when her eye had been injured in the attempt on her father's life.

'Time for bed,' said Louis as he appeared from the doorway carrying a glass of orange juice. 'I have to examine your eyes tomorrow and I want them wide open. I have to see you early as I have other matters that can't wait, and when those are done we can ride together.' He handed the glass to the child and watched her drink all the juice. 'Angela will put you to bed, and you needn't get up until I am ready for you. Have a good long rest. It's very late,' he added, smiling, as if he shared her delight in being up so late.

Aysha giggled and put her hand in Angela's. 'Louis is—what do you say? Bossy!'

'Go and say goodnight to your mother and I'll read to you for a while in bed,' Angela promised. She glanced up at Louis, who seemed to tower over her as he stood close and she smelled the expensive cologne and the subtle masculine scent of a healthy virile male. 'I'll say goodnight too,' she said, as calmly as she could through dry lips. 'I'll stay until Aysha is asleep and then go to bed. I'll be ready for you in the morning as I can have the trolley laid up before Aysha wakes. Do they know that she must have no breakfast?'

'That's why we shall do this as early as possible. I gave her a sleeping draught in that drink and she'll sleep until we fetch her in the morning. We can promise her breakfast after the examination and say that I am in a big hurry.'

Louis looked at the gold Rolex on his wrist. 'Don't go to bed yet. I have two calls to make and one to receive, and then we must talk.'

'I can't take any more tonight, Louis.' Angela felt weary and sad. 'You talk in riddles. Dermot hasn't bothered to phone me and I don't know what's happening, and to tell you the truth I just don't care!'

'I think you do,' he said quietly.

She took Aysha by the hand as the girl came across the room to them. 'Goodnight. I'm going to bed as soon as Aysha is asleep,' Angela said clearly.

'Coward,' he whispered, and bent to kiss Aysha on the brow. He touched Angela's hand briefly, squeezing the fingers and making her tremble inwardly.

Two phones calls? she wondered. One at least from the girl he was about to marry, and yet he had shown that he expected Angela to fall into his arms on any terms he might like to suggest. Her heart ached with a wanton desire that made her glad to be safe with the child she had in her care. Tonight, with the sound of Tunisian music in her ears and the sea murmuring over the dark sand, she could never have said no to anything he suggested, if he touched her, held her close and let his passion harden into lust.

The heavy silk of the *haik* was sensuous and did nothing to hide the allure of a good body, and once safe in her room she let it slip from her body to leave her free of its enchantment. She knew it had been a great mistake to wear it. The emeralds gleamed as she put them back into the velvet-lined box and slipped it into a drawer. I'll return them all tomorrow and forget that I ever wore fancy dress to look like a creature to be desired and used, she thought, and smiled reluctantly. To imagine herself as the kind of woman that Muslim men think they will find supplied for them in heaven was really amusing. Were they rationed to one, or could they have as many as they liked?

And so she had slept deeply but with strange dreams and woke early to find tea by her side and a smiling girl pulling back the window curtains. She dressed and went to Aysha, who murmured sleepily and showed no signs of wanting to get up. Angela smiled. The drug must have been potent and she knew that Aysha would have no idea of what was happening. She didn't even notice that the patch of local anaesthetic was strapped to her hand.

And now Angela started as Mohammed said something. 'I'm sorry, I was thinking about the instruments,' she said. 'I've checked and we're quite ready, so I'll fetch Aysha.'

'I will carry her,' said Mohammed. 'I carry her if they bring her back in the plane late and she is sleepy, and she will not question it.' They smiled, knowing that they were both fond of the little girl. 'Afterwards, she will no longer have the sign of the evil eye?' he asked anxiously.

'She will have straight eyes and much beauty,'

said Angela gravely. 'I will call the doctor, and then come with you.'

'Sleepyhead,' said Angela, and Aysha turned her back on them. 'If you're so tired and lazy, perhaps Mohammed ought to carry you, as we can't keep Louis waiting,' Angela said, sitting on the bed and laughing. 'What a lovely baby you are!'

Aysha smiled. 'Carry me,' she said, and put up her arms. 'Maman says I am too big now to be carried, but I like it.'

Mohammed laughed. 'You have eaten too many sweets, and I am not so strong, but I will try.' Gently he lifted her from the bed and carried her down to the operating-room, placing her on the couch outside the screen. It was going to be easier than they had expected. The hidden tensions that the child suffered could have erupted and caused her distress. Angela saw the fingernails bitten down to the quicks, that showed how affected she had been by the attack, and she was filled with tenderness for her little friend.

'I'll see where Dr Joudet is,' she whispered as Aysha snuggled down on the couch and closed her eyes again.

She asked a boy who was sweeping the terrace and he pointed to the study window. Angela went inside and ran to the half-open door.

He was talking to someone on the telephone. 'I'm happy for you. Did everything go off well? You are sure you really did make the right decision?' He paused and listened and then went on, 'I was certain that it was right for you. If we believe in what we do, we must go ahead and do what is right, even if it hurts others at times. Try to feel no guilt, and make a home of love and happiness. I wish you many lovely children.' He listened again and laughed, with a throaty warmth that told how sincere he was. 'Yes, I hope to do the same soon. Your example gives me hope for my own future. Goodbye, my dear little Yasmin. Bless you for having the courage to choose the right man.'

'I'm sorry,' Angela apologised. 'I didn't know. . .'

'That was Yasmin, my sister.' He smiled. 'She was married yesterday. I couldn't say anything until it was over, but now she is married and safe, no other person can untie that knot and interfere. She sounds very happy and I'm sure made the right choice.'

'Your sister is married?'

He nodded and went towards the door. 'I'll tell you about it later, but now I assume that Aysha is ready for me? I had hoped to talk to you last night, but you didn't reappear.'

'Aysha is sleepy and everything is ready. I'll wait with her until she's under.' It was a relief to concentrate on the work in hand and to forget that Yasmin had married the man chosen for her and didn't regret it. Now Louis could do the same, with all doubts dispelled and his duty clear.

The anaesthetist pulled back the strapping over the now numbed skin and carefully injected the first anaesthetic. Aysha sagged gently and Angela held her jaw while the pillow under her shoulder was taken away. The laryngeal tube slid back into her throat and was connected with the apparatus, making the unconscious state complete, light but relaxed, and Aysha was transferred to the operating table.

Swiftly Angela put on her own mask and scrubbed her hands, then shrugged into the gown held for her. She went up to the table and looked down at the now pale face of the girl who breathed easily and deeply and had no fears of what was happening.

'Does she really need this done?' she asked impulsively.

Louis glanced at the bubble in the anaesthetic machine monitor and waited for the signal that Aysha was fully relaxed and the operation could go ahead. 'I know some people think that a slight squint is attractive and some men find it irresistible, but if she is to mix with other Africans and maybe fall in love with a man from a culture that distrusts what they think is a sign of the evil eye, then she would be very unhappy later in life, and it could leave a scar on her mind for ever once she was scorned for being slightly different.'

'I noticed that she was a bit long-sighted for a child, and finds close-up print hard to read. Has this anything to do with the squint?'

Angela watched while Louis selected a small slender blade and made a tiny incision at the side of the affected eye so that he could reach the muscle holding the eyeball under too much tension. 'Very observant,' he said. 'She has a slight problem which can be controlled with contact lenses if she really needs them, but this particular squint wasn't the cause of it. I think she had a knock when she fell from a pony and the muscle was bruised. The squint came soon after that, I believe, but I wasn't here and didn't see Aysha when she was a small child.' He sighed and bent over the still form, delicately raising the taut muscle with a strabismus hook and then incising the muscle tendon with a tenetome to release it. He looked at both eyes and examined the tension in the good muscle of the unaffected eye.

'That should do it,' he said at last. 'Such pretty eyes, and yet Vassila was frightened and wouldn't let me near the child when she was younger. One day I saw her by accident and accused the parents of keeping her from the treatment she should have had several years ago.'

'But they're so fond of you,' Angela said.

'I got to know them well and made sure that Aysha trusted me.' He glanced at Angela as she handed him the tiny atraumatic needle and silk thread with which he proceeded to stitch the outer incision. 'I love the child as if she was my own, and I hope that one day I shall have children who will fill my life with laughter.'

Angela handed him a swab to clean away a bead of blood from the stitches and dared not look directly at him. He wanted children like Aysha with dark eyes and plump small hands and the lively nature of the Tunisian child. A woman like the one he had held so tenderly in his arms could give him such children even if he wasn't truly in love with her, and with friendship and affection, passion would follow and deepen.

'A pad for each eye,' said Louis. 'Make the one covering the unaffected eye small so that she can see out at the sides until she is fully awake. I did warn her that I might put pads on her eyes after the drops and examination, so she may remember, but we don't want her scared if she wakes and can't see.'

'But she'll have pads over both eyes for two days, I suppose?' asked Angela.

'That's right, and stitches out in six days.' He grinned and she saw his eyes glinting over the mask. 'After that, there will be exercises to teach her, and so, Sister Menzies, you must make up your mind that you have to stay with us for a little longer.'

The anaesthetist smiled and removed the laryngeal tube. Already Aysha stirred and mumbled in her sleep as the light anaesthetic released her back to consciousness. Mohammed, who had remained in the room during the operation as if on guard, now gathered her up and carried her to her room, and Angela took off her mask and followed them. Qucikly she pulled the curtains across the windows and shut out the glare. Angela sat with her until she opened her eyes and peeped out of the side of the small eye-pad.

'Hello! You're awake! While we had you fast asleep it seemed a good idea to do that small operation that needed to be done before you go away to school,' Angela explained.

'But I didn't know! I felt nothing! It didn't hurt.'

'Now I must bandage the other eye for a few hours just to rest the muscles,' Angela told her, 'and

then you'll have eyes that look straight ahead when
you next see your mother. Louis wants you to sleep
a lot, and then there'll be exercises to learn.' She
put the double pads on and made them comfortable.

'You won't leave me, Angela?'

'Azziza will sit with you and call me if you want
anything. When you're less sleepy, I'll read to you,
and your mother will come later to sit with you too.'
Angela saw that Aysha was nearly asleep again. 'I
shall pin a note to the bed, telling everyone to speak
before they touch the bed so that you'll know when
they're there.'

The Arab girl sat by the window, content to wait
until she was told to go away. She looked tranquil,
and when Louis came into the room Angela whispered, 'She's so patient.'

'Patient and devoted,' Louis said. 'We can wait
for anything we want with devotion and tenacity if
it's something we really want.' He touched a tendril
of hair on the cheek of the sleeping child. 'She can
go away now when she is ready for school and mix
with anyone and make friends,' he said. They
walked from the room, and he stretched and
laughed softly.

'Did you sleep?' asked Angela.

'Yes, and I feel wonderful. I woke early and
thought of my sister and was full of happiness.'

'I hope she's very happy,' Angela said politely as
she would about anyone she didn't really know. It
sounded empty, like a greeting between strangers.

'I forgot that you haven't met her,' said Louis.
'She was in Sousse a few days ago when you were

there. We must have been in the hotel at the same time but just didn't get together. She needed me to give her courage for what she had to do. Of course, she is away now, but you must meet her soon.'

'I doubt if that will happen. Aysha will have no need of me and I shall go back to London.'

'Rubbish! You have three more weeks here.' He laughed at her amazement. 'Didn't I tell you that you're engaged here for the full six weeks that your other cases would have covered?'

'No, you did not, and I'm sure you're mistaken. The director of the agency would never let me waste time like that,' Angela assured him.

He put a hand into an inner pocket and produced a letter. She turned it over. It was hand-delivered, but it was in the official envelope of the agency. 'A diplomatic bag comes in useful,' he said. 'Postal services here are not all that good and I asked them to send your mail through the Embassy.'

She opened it and found her salary cheque up to the end of the week and a note to say that they expected her to report back at the end of a further three weeks. 'I don't understand,' she said.

'Last night I wanted to talk, but you walked out on me,' Louis told her.

'I didn't! I was tired.'

'You were scared.' Her eyelashes fluttered down like twin moths. 'You knew that you were far too attractive for any man to resist, and even though you accepted and wore my gifts, you kept away.' His face lost its light-hearted expression. 'Did I offend you by taking your cause personally? Did you feel that I had no right to defend you?'

Vassila came into the study in a flurry of excitement. 'I have seen her and she sleeps like a baby. How can I ever thank you?'

'It was a very minor operation,' Louis pointed out, smiling.

'To you, yes, but to me, after everything that has happened, it was important that she shouldn't be hurt again, and yet it had to be done as she grows into a woman soon and must go to school to take her away from men until she marries.' Vassila's eyes filled with tears. 'I am selfish. I have taken so much of your time, and I know you want to show our country to Angela.' She smiled. 'You said you wanted to go to Hammamet. I have ordered a small lunch and then you can see Aysha once more before you go for the rest of the day.' She laughed. 'I think it wise that you are not here when your mother telephones again. If you are unavailable, even she cannot contact you.'

'You are right—it wouldn't help anyone if I talked to her now,' said Louis. 'She leaves for France tomorrow, and once she is among French friends she will be comforted and the pain will be less. I'm very sorry for her, but Yasmin must have her own life, without her interference.'

Angela went to change into a light dress and sandals. What was happening? Nobody explained, and Vassila obviously thought she knew more than she did. I give up, she thought with a wry smile. If Yasmin has married the man picked out for her, then surely her mother could let her go? Surely she wouldn't want to go on the honeymoon with the couple? She couldn't rule them as much as that! Perhaps it had been a civil marriage as Yasmin was half French and it was done so quickly. That could offend the orthodox Muslim lady, who might have wanted a lot of fuss and a great feast.

Today, I must remember everything and take away a few precious memories, Angela decided, and one day I may read in the marriage columns that Dr Jean-Louis Husain Joudet has married a woman I shall never know, but whose gentle face I can never hate.

CHAPTER NINE

THERE was no way of refusing to go with Louis. Vassila hovered over them and rushed them through lunch and waved as they went off in the car. Angela tried to stay with Aysha, but the child was asleep and there was no need for anyone but the girl sitting by the window to stay in the room with her, so at last she had to join Louis and leave the house.

Now I shall have to listen to his plans and pretend to be pleased, she thought. I just hope he doesn't suggest that I'm set up in a nice little apartment as his girlfriend after he's married! I shall either hit him or fall into his arms! Angela stole a glance at the strong handsome face and couldn't read his mind.

'The car is a bit less dusty than it was the last time I travelled with you,' she remarked. It was shining, and the interior was brushed and sweet-smelling with tiny vases of orange blossom on the back ledge.

'It had travelled a very long way that night,' he said. 'It was a long night for many people.'

'Am I allowed to know anything now? What did happen that night?' Angela needed to know and yet dreaded what she might hear. 'I heard voices in Dermot's room but didn't see him again. The "Do not disturb" slip was on the door in the morning, and I didn't go in to say goodbye.' She looked puzzled. 'Of course, he might not have been there. I just don't know if he left and came back in the early hours, but Dermot isn't the type to slip off to a nightclub without me. He said he was much too tired and needed his beauty sleep. He left no message and I couldn't get him on the phone today.' She felt resentful. 'It isn't like Dermot to do anything unpredictable. What happened to Karl? I never did see him, although there was a room booked for him. Was he even in Tunis, or was he too upset to face you after your sister made up her mind to marry?'

'All those empty beds seem to bother you,' Louis laughed. 'Can't you get away from bed numbers even in a hotel, but want to fill them with people under your care as you would in hospital? You had a room all to yourself with plenty of space as it had two beds in it,' he remarked. 'Dermot had a room and so did Karl. I should know, as I booked them.'

Angela blinked. A double room booked for her by Louis Joudet? Dermot would never allow a man to share her room, under his nose, if that was what Louis had intended.

'Just why was that room booked for me?' she asked with a dangerous gleam in her eyes.

'We thought my sister might have to share with you. She couldn't wander about Tunis without a chaperon, and you were there as Dermot suggested. He thought it would solve a lot of problems in case the Press came along and snooped on us all.'

'I see,' she said, but she didn't.

Louis avoided a herd of goats that wandered

across the road followed by the oldest man that Angela had ever seen. He waved a long staff in contempt of the vehicle that tried to disrupt the passage along the road that had been used by goatherds for hundreds of years. He spat into the shadow of the car as it passed, cursing the infidels who rode in it but only as a habitual gesture, then went on his way, like a painting from the Old Testament.

A long hedge of cactus cast a dark shadow on the white road and at intervals stalls containing hundreds of fresh oranges of enormous size made brief splashes of colour against the ochre earth and whitewashed houses. Colours and the ever-present music lulled her into a sense of mild enjoyment. Why not enjoy the company of this man for a little while? The sense of history was around her, the pace of life slow and the fatalistic attitude of the people in the villages was the same as it had been for centuries, and it was impossible to ignore it and not be influenced by the slow pace and tranquillity. She exclaimed at one huge heap of oranges, and Louis stopped the car to buy some that had cool dark leaves still attached to the fruit, and handed her a spray of orange blossom that the man had put among the oranges.

They left the car in Hammamet and wandered through time in the narrow streets and below the overhang of upper windows. Small shops held treasures of filigree silver, beaten brass and beautiful carpets. A showroom for pottery stood out as

more modern, and beyond it Angela saw the work-
shops where the pots were made.

A man invited them in, and they saw tiny children
trampling the clay in a deep trough to soften it,
other older children moulding certain shapes that
would become plates and shallow dishes, and others
were painting lines and simple leaf shapes on dishes.
The senior members of the family fashioned exquisite lampshades similar to the ones beneath the roof
of the terrace at Sidi, where tiny birds made nests
among the intricate fretwork of the baked clay. The
display of brilliant birds took her breath away. She
saw a huge version of the cockerel she had bought
and which now sat on her dressing-table. It stood
high on a plinth and she was enchanted, but had to
turn away as it was far too heavy to take back to
London. She bought several small presents for
people back home and asked what she could buy for
Dermot. 'I'd like to send a gift to Karl too,' she
suggested, thinking it might cheer him up.

'Something for Karl, yes, but do you think
Dermot would use an ornament?'

'No,' she admitted. 'He isn't very artistic and
never notices his surroundings if he's fed and has a
bed to sleep on, but they share the same quarters,
and Karl might like something bright,' she said.

'Not any more,' Louis told her. 'Dermot will have
his bungalow to himself for a while. For the next
few weeks until they have bought a villa, Karl will
live in a very luxurious caravan in the oasis near the
mine.' Angela stared. 'A married man can't leave
his wife a week after the wedding and sleep alone in

a mining camp!' He laughed and his face was suddenly full of mischief. 'You really haven't guessed, have you? Karl and Yasmin were married in the German Embassy the other night.'

'All that whispering was you and Karl and Dermot and Yasmin geting together to leave for the Embassy?'

'She's got it!' he said in mock admiration, and laughed at her bemused expression.

'You said you had an emergency,' she accused him, and was empty of all feeling. 'They didn't tell me. I was left out, and even my dear brother who shares so much with me didn't have the decency to let me know what was going on!'

'What's more urgent than a man about to be married? He needed all the help we could give him, and I love my sister very much.' Louis saw her distress. 'You could do nothing, and it was better that as few people as possible were involved.'

'Oh,' she said in a small voice, and her heart beat faster, colour tinging her cheeks with pink. 'Are you and your sister rather alike in appearance?'

'If it wasn't for the four years between us we could be twins,' he said.

A veil lifted, but Angela couldn't believe it possible. 'I think I saw you together at the hotel,' she said slowly, and wondered why she had not noticed the resemblance that Yasmin had to her brother even when she had been distressed and needing his comforting arms about her. Her pulse beat heavily. 'You might have mentioned it before now,' she said stiffly. 'I feel a fool!'

'It had to be a secret until after the ceremony as my mother wanted to stop the marriage, and Yasmin was not ready to meet new friends. I went to see my mother and told her of my decision to let Yasmin marry Karl, in my position as head of the household.' Louis smiled grimly. 'That's not a stand I want to take and hope never to press it in future as I like everyone to make their own decisions, including my mother, but she was so sure that she wanted all the old customs and manners that I reminded her that if that is so, she couldn't rule us and I must make all the decisions in the family now, as a good Tunisian male would do.'

He sighed. 'I hated doing it, but when she recovers and talks to her French connections she will calm down; until then I am keeping away from her house.'

Louis selected a ceramic fish with every subtle colour of a fish's scales in the workmanship. It twisted upwards out of green waves as if leaping, and the potter had captured even the droplets of water on the body. 'I shall buy it for Karl,' he said. 'The fish is a sacred symbol that will remind him that his wife has another culture that must be revered as well as his own. It must blend with their lives and never make dissension between the two. That is important.' His eyes were brooding and he didn't meet her gaze.

Outside, the sun beat down in a harsher radiance than Angela remembered in the sunset. They strolled by the sea and watched a red-sailed *dhow* float across the calm water. The sailors on board were chanting, with one standing on the prow watching the distance for shoals of fish as evening came. The hot sand, the scent of spices, the music and the sea breeze could only have come from Africa, and Angela sighed. 'Vassila told me that once I'd smelled Tunisia and let the sands of the desert run through my fingers I would want to return,' she said quietly, and a great calm enfolded her.

They sat on a low wall in front of one of the huge hotels that lined the shore of Hammamet behind banks of vivid succulent plants in the gardens by the sea, and watched the sky trace the end of day in colours that made the heart ache with their beauty. 'And are you enchanted enough to return?' Louis asked.

'Who can tell?' queried Angela. 'Sometimes I feel I'm the only one who doesn't know what's happening here, and I was hurt to be excluded from what was happening. Even my own brother didn't tell me. This is a strange country and I don't know if it likes me. Some places choose and discard any who don't fit in.'

'It likes you,' Louis said simply.

'The desert covers all footsteps in time and forgets people who have been here. It would forget me in a week.'

He shook his head. 'You would be remembered.'

'I have no ties here,' she reminded him, 'except to Dermot, and he might well be in Peru next year!' She wore a secret smile and the dimple in her chin quivered with a hint of delicious realisation, as a glow began to warm her heart.

'If I asked you to come back, what would you say?'

'Do you want me to meet the woman chosen for you?' she asked demurely. She gazed out over the silken water and up to the burnished sky.

'I make my own choice,' he stated. 'My family knows it, and Yasmin would be my firm ally.' He moved away and took from his pocket a newspaper he had bought while Angela collected souvenirs. She recoiled as if it might attack her, her calm shattered and the spell broken. 'It's all right,' he said. 'I wanted to be sure it was done as I insisted it should be done. Read this and then forget it all, but read it first.'

'Is it there?' Angela asked.

'A full retraction and apology in Arabic, French and English.' He held it out, but she found it difficult to read in the dying light, and it wasn't only the dusk that dimmed her vision.

'I can't read it and I don't think I want to know what it says,' she averred. 'Please, Louis, can't we try to forget that this ever happened?'

'Listen,' he insisted. He read the retraction and the fact that an unspecified sum for damages had been settled out of court. The next paragraph had a statement that Shane Winsconsin had left the country after successful engine trials and was now with his fiancée in America.

Angela sighed, relieved that it was over. 'I didn't know he was engaged,' she said. 'Poor girl!'

'He's been quoted as engaged every time he needs to be painted whiter than white,' Louis said, laughing. 'Maybe there's a "Rent-a-fiancée" list somewhere of women who agree not to sue him for breach of promise.'

Angela saw that he had more to read and she paled at what might come now, but Louis continued, a pulse beating in his temple as if he was under stress. 'We would like to take this opportunity to wish Miss Menzies every happines when she marries one of our leading surgeons and businessmen, Dr Jean-Louis Husain Joudet, whose father will be long remembered as a faithful and good friend of Tunisia, who also became a subject of our country and married a member of one of our great families.'

'It can't say that!' A tiny flame of hope flickered into uncertain warmth as she looked at him with pleading in her tear-filled eyes. If this was a cruel joke, then she wanted to die. The flame gathered courage and steadied into a glow as he took her face between his hands and kissed her trembling lips.

'*Ma petite*,' he whispered into her hair. His fingers pulled at the fair strands until she was haloed in radiance. '*Mon amour*,' he murmured, and pulled her into his arms, his kisses taking away all thought, all resistance and all resolution. The force of his lean tense body against her made her melt into the fierce embrace that told him everything he needed to know or hear, of her heart and mind and love, and the sky held no star brighter than their eyes.

'I thought——' she began, but his kisses would not let her speak.

Why had she not noticed the resemblance between Louis and the girl he held so tenderly in the hotel, who must have been Yasmin? I saw only what I expected to see, she thought. Soft chanting across the bay told them of fish heavy and bright, silvering the nets, and they sat locked in each other's arms satiated with wonder and content after all the doubts and yearning.

'We must go,' he said at last. He smiled down at her, caressing her body and smoothing the locks of hair he had tousled.

'Yes, we must go before another camera finds us and then they'll know just how abandoned I can be.' Angela smiled and touched the corner of his mouth.

'Shall we stay here to eat? I can't drive back yet. Tonight we eat Tunisian food and then go back and tell Vassila our news.'

Angela looked alarmed. 'Wasn't it cruel to let them print that where your mother can read it?'

'I told my mother that I hoped to marry you, and by now she is on the way to France. As for Vassila, she is a very wise woman who never reads the newspapers and knows that this is fate and we are all in the hands of Allah. She took it for granted that you will stay and marry me. In fact she told me not to leave it for too long, as she disapproves of unmarried ladies wandering about in the dark with unmarried men who are not of the family. She has a very realistic view of men and their passions, and has no intention that Aysha shall ever be in danger from them. She will accept everything we plan and

say that we can now be useful and chaperon her
daughter when she goes to Europe to school, and
take her on a grand tour when she has holidays.' He
grinned. 'Never say that women here are under the
influence of others! They smile and sweetly rule
from the wings, and we shall find that Vassila has
what she wants in every way. How else would I
leave my patients to tend one small girl in Sidi?'

Angela laughed helplessly, light-headed with joy
and relief. 'She said you'd be useful when you were
married,' she recalled, 'but she didn't include me,
which I suppose was tactful as you hadn't even said
you loved me.'

'If we stay here, I shall think that Vassila is
looking over my shoulder. There is a time and
place, she would say, and regret it if we snatched
our love in out-of-the-way places.' Louis drew
Angela from the wall on which that sat. He kissed
her lips as if for the first time, lingering on their
softness and sighing as he released her. 'Come, my
love,' he said. 'Food and drink, and then we can
plan for the future.'

The hotel dining-room in the sprawling complex
behind the gardens looked far too bright and
modern and soulless, so they walked out into the
old town and found a small eating house behind the
market where the smell of couscous and braised
pigeons drew them to the table. Louis gave the
order in Arabic, which brought the full attention of
the proprietor, who served them fresh hot and spicy
food and cold fruit juice.

'Delicious,' Angela said at last. 'Falling in love

makes me hungry.' She laughed. 'Do you as a Frenchman prefer your women slender, or can I eat sweetmeats and grow fat like an Arab woman?'

'What a dilemma! When we go to Europe, you will have to go on a crash diet and then feed up when we are here again!'

They walked back to the car, and Angela knew she would think of this night as long as she lived, with the smell of orange blossom in the car and the sharper scent of the ripe fruit in the back seat, and Louis, adoring and somehow as if she had known him before, in another life, another time, his remembered kisses on her lips, and her body softened in anticipation of love.

'Tomorrow I shall telephone your Embassy and make arrangements for our wedding,' Louis told her when they were once more in the dimly lit salon, now deserted and clear of all traces of the evening's entertainment. 'Ali will be of use there, and I can bear to wait no longer, my darling.' A servant came to the archway leading to the hall and then went away as silently as he had come. 'You see? Vassila checks that we are safely home and are not alone on the beach! You must marry me now. We are hopelessly compromised!'

'Hopelessly,' Angela agreed.

'We must look at Aysha before we rest,' Louis said. 'If only to see that she is not stifled by care and attention.'

The room was dark, with just a small lamp burning in one corner away from the bed, and a woman sat as if carved from stone, alert and smiling as they entered and peeped at the girl on the bed.

'Has she been awake?' asked Angela, and the woman nodded.

'Is that you, Angela?' Aysha struggled to sit up, but Louis gently put her back on the one pillow allowed her.

'I'm here, and so is Louis. You must sleep, and then after tomorrow, you can throw away the eye-pads for ever.'

Aysha put out a hand and Angela held it. 'I dreamed that you had gone away. You must stay with us for ever, Angela.'

'Yes, I shall stay,' Angela said quietly. 'You can be the first to know. Louis and I are going to get married.'

Aysha felt the emerald ring that had found its way on to Angela's engagement finger some time during the magic evening. 'I know that. Maman told me a long time ago that it would be so, but now you wear the ring to say it, and so I can talk about it too.'

Angela shook her head in mock despair, then bent to kiss the child goodnight. 'Was this your idea, or did Vassila tell you to marry me?' she asked as they walked away.

'All my own idea, but Vassila did say that no man walked in the dark, unchaperoned with an unmarried girl, unless he was to marry her. That really did seal my fate,' Louis said, teasing her.

'And now?' Her eyes were bright and her breath

came in shallow uneven bursts as he took her hand
and led her towards her room.

'Now I am awake and we must watch the dawn.'
He smiled as a softly shod servant bowed and set a
tray of coffee on the low table by the window to the
terrace. 'Vassila again.' He spoke to the man and
told him to go to bed, and at last the huge house
was quiet and there were no eyes to watch them.

'If I drink any more coffee, I shall lie awake for
hours,' Angela said. He filled her cup again and
laughed softly. 'I really should get some sleep,' she
said.

'Later.' The word hung on the air. 'What is time?'
he asked. '"Unborn tomorrow and dead yesterday.
Why fret about them if today be sweet!"'

He pushed aside the cups and led her to her room
where the wide window looked over the dark sea
and the fading lights of the village. 'Tomorrow we
make arrangements for a wedding between a
Frenchman and an English girl, with all the sophisticated trimmings of the twentieth century, but
tonight I want to watch the dawn with you wearing
the *haik*.'

Angela nodded and watched him leave the room,
then changed quickly, the silken garment clinging to
her warm naked body and her hair loose and soft
over her shoulders. She sat by the window, and
gasped when Louis came back, dressed in a white
gondura, dominant and dark in the half light.

He held her close and their bodies were apart by
only a wisp of fabric and the silken *haik*. Angela
clung to him as they kissed, his mouth searching for

her mouth, her eyelids and the soft folds of her throat. Her body was limp with desire and she knew that he would be magnificent. A great white shadow engulfed her as the *haik* slipped to the floor and revealed her body in all its tender submission. With a cry that was as old as the desert, Louis took her, carefully and with restraint, making her moan with delight and pain, and her tears made dewdrops on his broad brown chest.

In the distance, she heard the first sign of the dawn, the *muezzin* calling the faithful to prayer, and then the sound that would make her smile tenderly whenever she heard it, the sound of the cockerel crowing his triumph at another night of darkness, defeated by the dawn.

— MEDICAL ♥ ROMANCE —

The books for your enjoyment this month are:

EASTERN ADVENTURE Lisa Cooper
DANGEROUS PRACTICE Sheila Danton
ENTER DR JONES Judith Hunte
THE CURE FOR LONELINESS Jennifer Eden

♥   ♥   ♥   ♥   ♥

Treats in store!

Watch next month for the following absorbing stories:

A DREAM WORTH SHARING Hazel Fisher
GIVE BACK THE YEARS Elisabeth Scott
UNCERTAIN FUTURE Angela Devine
REPEAT PRESCRIPTION Sonia Deane

Available from Boots, Martins, John Menzies, W.H. Smith, Woolworths and other paperback stockists.

Also available from Reader Service, P.O. Box 236, Thornton Road, Croydon, Surrey CR9 3RU.

Readers in South Africa — write to:
Independent Book Services Pty, Postbag X3010, Randburg, 2125, S. Africa.

A
SPECIAL GIFT
FOR
MOTHER'S DAY

Four new Romances by some of your favourite authors have been selected as a special treat for Mother's Day.

A CIVILISED
ARRANGEMENT
Catherine George
THE GEMINI BRIDE
Sally Heywood
AN IMPOSSIBLE
SITUATION
Margaret Mayo
LIGHTNING'S LADY
Valerie Parv

Four charming love stories for only £5.80, the perfect gift for Mother's Day . . . or you can even treat yourself.

Look out for the special pack from January 1991.

Discover the thrill of 4 Exciting Medical Romances – FREE

BOOKS FOR YOU

In the exciting world of modern
medicine, the emotions of true love
have an added drama. Now you can
experience four of these
unforgettable romantic tales of passion
and heartbreak FREE – and look forward to
a regular supply of Mills & Boon
Medical Romances delivered direct to your door!

🍂 🍂 🍂

Turn the page for details of 2 extra
free gifts, and how to apply.

An Irresistible Offer from Mills & Boon

Here's an offer from Mills & Boon to become a regular reader of Medical Romances. To welcome you, we'd like you to have four books, a cuddly teddy and a special MYSTERY GIFT, all absolutely free and without obligation.

Then, every month you could look forward to receiving 4 more **brand new** Medical Romances for £1.45 each, delivered direct to your door, post and packing free. Plus our newsletter featuring author news, competitions, special offers, and lots more.

This invitation comes with no strings attached. You can cancel or suspend your subscription at any time, and still keep your free books and gifts.

Its so easy. Send no money now. Simply fill in the coupon below and post it at once to -

**Mills & Boon Reader Service, FREEPOST,
PO Box 236, Croydon, Surrey CR9 9EL**

NO STAMP REQUIRED

✂ -

YES! Please rush me my 4 Free Medical Romances and 2 Free Gifts! Please also reserve me a Reader Service Subscription. If I decide to subscribe, I can look forward to receiving 4 brand new Medical Romances every month for just £5.80, delivered direct to my door. Post and packing is free, and there's a free Mills & Boon Newsletter. If I choose not to subscribe I shall write to you within 10 days - I can keep the books and gifts whatever I decide. I can cancel or suspend my subscription at any time. I am over 18.

EP03D

Name (Mr/Mrs/Ms) _____

Address _____

_____

_____ Postcode _____

Signature _____

The right is reserved to refuse an application and change the terms of this offer. Offer expires **July 31st 1991**. Readers in Southern Africa write to P.O. Box 2125, Randburg, South Africa. Other Overseas and Eire, send for details. You may be mailed with other offers from Mills & Boon and other reputable companies as a result of this application. If you would prefer not to share in this opportunity, please tick box. ☐